Leo and Journey Into the Multiverse

The Delve For Hades

SCYTHAN E.

PARTRIDGE

To order additional copies of this book, contact
Toll Free 800 101 2657 (Singapore)
Toll Free 1 800 81 7340 (Malaysia)
orders.singapore@partridgepublishing.com

www.partridgepublishing.com/singapore

CONTENTS

PART 1

Leo and the Delve for Hades

(Years After the Incident)

A few years ago, Leo lost a part of his life - his best friend, companion and sidekick, Hades, who sacrificed himself to save Leo and the rest of the Empyreans to prevent the demon armada from destroying the Intergalactic Federation on Xenia and the rest of the galaxies. Thought to have perished in the Incident, the Empyrean Spirit, Empyrea, suggested otherwise and gave the word that he was still alive somewhere. However, the only thing she provided Leo was a hint to begin their search to find Hades, leaving it up to him and the remaining Empyreans to figure out everything from scratch.

Leo strived to find his long lost companion, his hope and determination to find Hades was still blazing like fire. Seeking the help of his sciencey associate and genius inventor of the Intergalactic Federation, "Paws" Paulson, he began his search to find him using all of the Xenian technologies available to him to detect track down any traces of Hades' Empyrean signal they could find in the universe.

Nearly a decade after Hades' disappearance, much has changed, especially for the five remaining Empyreans. Throughout the passing years, with the futuristic technological advancements readily provided to them by the Federation, their day-to-day lives improved. Occasionally, there would be missions assigned to the

Empyreans, to bring peace to many and justice to those who attempt to tip over the scales of balance, extending past their limitations and developing stronger Empyrean abilities.

As they grew, so did the Federation's leader and Leo's foster father, Basileus, in his age that is. Growing old and frail, he eventually bequeathed his leadership to another and left Xenia, dawning upon the new age for the growth of the Federation.

Chapter 1

(The Dimensional Delver)

Years flew past like pages of the book as if destiny was leafing through it, decades since the Empyreans' major accomplishment coupled with a devastating blow from the loss of a teammate in what they call, the Incident. They waited for a sign, something that could eventually pave a way to Hades. Every now and then, they would meet up in the Federation's Nexus building rooftop garden to bide their time by leisurely catching-up with each other. On one of those days, in particular, Leo was early and the leaned onto the cold metallic railings of the garden balcony, staring at all the flying vehicles that whizzed past the side of the building.

Leo sighed as he thought more about Hades and wondered whether something would come as an optimistic turnaround to his dwindling patience and yearning to be able to see him again, one of the things that ailed him from the day of loss. He felt unmoored and had gnawing worries running through his head, namely, 'why did he do it?' He glanced over at his holographic-watch intermittently to check for the time while he waited. Slowly, as the minutes ticked by, Kadyn showed up silently and settled her arm onto his shoulder.

"You're early."

He looked up to see the familiar pair of hazel coloured piercing eyes and immediately turned back down to staring at the flying cars. "Still worried about losing Hades, aren't you, honey?"

"Yeah... After all these years since the Incident, so much has changed that has been bringing me down. It's true I've been thinking about him a lot lately and how he prevented me from saving him using my own powers."

"I think it's just meant to be as predestined, written with permanent ink on a blank paper. He did what he thought was righteous, in a sense," Kadyn wrapped her arms around Leo's torso and hugged him from behind, leaning her head on his back. "He's a selfless one and should be powerful enough to manage himself if he's still somewhere out there. One day, we might actually see him again."

"You sound just like Empyrea with her spiritual talks," he remarked, leaving them in an explosive guffaw for a while.

"But on a serious note, I've been visiting Spiritus lately to learn some of the spiritual wisdom from her to straighten up my life from my turbulent past," Kadyn shared, nudging him gently on his gut and faced each other, bringing themselves into an intimate hug. As they hugged, they gradually inched their faces closer and closer, when...

"Ahem!" Kyudo cleared his throat as he arrived shortly after with the other Empyreans, interrupting their moment as he caught them off guard. "The cavalry has arrived!"

"Hey, ya two lovebirds! Weather's fine for some chemistry, ain't it?" Seiche exclaimed in addition to what he said, leaving the duo to blush in embarrassment. "And Leo, I know you're still missin' that li'l dude, just know you've got us coverin' ya tail. We'll try to find somethin' that we could cheer ya up until we reunite with that li'l fuzz."

Leo wished that something would happen to begin his search at that moment, something of great adventure other than just fighting wars for the Xenians. And soon enough, as though his thoughts were heard, Paulson contacted all of the Empyreans through their Holowatches to assemble at the laboratories of the

Federation, spreading the good news that someone had discovered Hades' Empyrean signature somewhere.

As soon as the words reach his ears, his eyes lit up with joy and he . Then and there, with all the excitement and hope welled up in him, Leo forgot about all his powers that allowed him to teleport instantaneously and sprinted through the corridor towards the laboratories, followed closely behind by the rest of the Empyreans who just ran along with him.

At the doors of the laboratories, Paulson welcomed them and brought them into the deep underground sections to meet another fellow scientist of the Federation. As they exited the laboratory lift, they were welcomed by a surprising sight. The scientist they were brought to was a white mouse in a white lab coat and glasses, and a third of Leo's height, standing on a step ladder just to match their height to see eye to eye so that they could talk.

"Hello, Empyreans. My name is Wensleydale Mousse Hamilton, or you could call me Wendale or Dale in short. I'm a Dimensional Delver, one who specialises in interdimensional travels and Multiverse delving research. As you might have known, I've managed to locate a powerful Empyrean life signature in another dimension and thought it might be your friend. If you want, I could take all of you there to find him. But first, before you travel through the dimensions, you need to know the prerequisite basics of the Science of Dimensions 101."

He cleared his throat for a moment and took in a deep breath.

"The Multiverse itself is made out of dimensions, each of a concentric plane of reality that..." Wendale started his lengthy rigmarole about the dimensions in his squeaky voice while the rest anticipated a lecture, swallowing in certain fear the instant he began speaking. However, they were lost in his words while he droned on.

"Argh! That's too complicated for us. Please put it in layman's terms for us to understand," Ignis voiced out in confusion, flustered by Wendale's words as he went over his head and what she heard was pure gibberish which could be comprehensible by those who were scientifically literate. The others gawked at him, still partially discombobulated about the science behind dimensions.

He then began to describe it in simple terms that the Multiverse is like a cluster of bubbles on a sort of dimensional ocean, which was also known as the Multiverse. Each bubble would represent individual dimensions, connected solely on the curved boundaries of each other called Cusps. To cross the Cusps, it required an intense source of energy in specific points of every dimension. This stopped him dead in his tracks in his research on dimensions until he discovered the Cuspmium crystals, a sporadically found crystalline structure capable of puncturing holes through the fabric of space in the form of temporary rifts to allow anyone to delve through the Cusps without harm.

"With Paws' help, we invented a remote interdimensional device and coined them as the Transdimensional Cuspers, or simply Cuspers in short. The discovery of the revolutionary, rapid interdimensional travel was accomplished by yours truly - the first Xenian to ever explore more dimensions in rapid succession throughout the Multiverse. As time went on, I recruited others to join me and we called ourselves, the Dimensional Delvers, the ones who've delved deep into the Multiverse and dedicated their lives to studying the unique worlds we visit."

As he took a breather from his incessant prattling, Paulson, who had been waiting patiently by his side, proceeded to show them to the Cuspers. He took out a silver briefcase with an illuminated holographic number pad and meticulously type in the password while mumbling each number and letter as he went along, eventually opening up to reveal multiple wristband devices, all varying hues of colour, set in foam to cushion them inside. He informed them that the Federation leader has already granted him permission to let them use the Cuspers for the search and for keeping afterwards.

"They can do what your Holowatch could ever do and more. It doubles as an interdimensional communicator and has a Multiverse Pathfinder so that you can locate the Cusps, or each other easily if you're lost. Just pick a colour and I can upgrade your Holowatches shortly afterwards."

Upon picking their preferred colours, Paulson instructed them to leave their chosen Cusper of choice with their corresponding Holowatches on his workbench. After placing their respective pairs of items down, he began using his convoluted tools and machinery to transfer information from the Holowatches to the Cuspers, leaving time for the Empyreans to loiter around the laboratory.

While the others stayed in the laboratory to wait, Leo decided to stroll around the gardens close by to take a break from Wendale's science "lecture" and sought for further wisdom from Empyrea before the search.

"Empyrea, if you're out there, I really need to know something," he shouted out towards the skies.

Instantaneously, Empyrea appeared in a burst of light as a spectral projection before she physically appeared, leaving him startled for a moment.

"Must you do that every time you come?"

"If need be. Xenia's a few light-years away from my home, so travelling here requires me to do this," she said with a pause, "what would you like to know, Leo? I sense uncertainty in you."

"You've said before that I could use my Empyrean powers to manipulate space and time, and Hades is in one of the other dimensions. So, does interdimensional travel count in as one of the Empyrean abilities of my powers?"

She nodded. "Yes, but alas, this is the last aspect of your powers that I cannot teach. Through trials and tribulations, resolving the conflict that resides in *you*, only *you* can help yourself to utilize it in future. As you know, I cannot interfere with how destiny unfurls. Only time will tell..." She streaked up into the sky and disappeared instantaneously, leaving Leo with pieces of wisdom he did not quite understand yet.

With an ambiguous answer given to him in response, he returned back to the laboratory and the first thing that caught his attention was Ignis in her new pink jumpsuit. "Lo and behold! I'm an official Dimensional Delver!" She posed with her pink Cusper in her right paw in the air.

"What's with the new outfit?"

"Leo, lemme give you a quick explanation," Wendale stepped in to answer, holding up a grey-coloured suit tessellated with tiny hexagonal patterns. "Before Paws asked all of you to the lab, he prepared these to help you and the rest of the Empyreans during the dimensional delving. These are special, thin and durable electro-fibre nano-tech suits designed for all kinds of adversities. The nanites weaved into the suit facilitates core temperature regulation in any climate through instantaneous acclimatisation and it has a customisable appearance of both colour and design."

With a pause to show Leo by flipping it front and back, he continued not too long after. "There are also transponder chips to track where you are in the Multiverse from Xenia and a built-in universal voice translator around the collar for effortless communication with beings of other worlds. It's nifty for wearable technology if I should say so myself. Here's yours. Go ahead and try it on," he babbled on for a while, gesticulating with his paws as he described it. Eventually, he passed it to Leo after finishing his long-winded explanation.

"And take your Cusper too!" Ignis added and passed his personal blue Cusper to him.

After a few minutes, he emerged from changing equipped with everything he needed, readily prepared to delve. Wendale asked if Paulson wanted to tag along but he declined as he preferred to stay in the laboratories to reorganise the Xenian data catalogues.

Thereafter, Wendale then took them outside to test out their holographic displays on the Cuspers to get used to the new systems, eventually instructing them on how to activate the display of the Multiverse map and its database. Upon activation, it displayed circles of different colours, markings, and labels, representing each dimension and brief information about what was in them.

While they explored the functionalities of the Cuspers, Wendale mumbled to himself and scrupulously checked off items in his holographic checklist. "Hmm, Empyrean Energy Signature

Detector functioning as normal, check. Cuspers functional, check. Cuspmium charges..." He paused for a moment hesitantly before he continued. "Should be fine for now..." When he was done with his checklist, he turned back to the Empyreans.

Wendale informed them that they were in Dimension 622, indicated by the cyan numbers on the top of the Cuspers' holographic display, and where they were headed to was Dimension 625, according to the Xenian Dimensional Database.

"The Pathfinder function points to the coordinates of the Cusp to be used as a delving spot for transitional travelling, or to locate your lost friends if that happens in any case. With the use of each Cusper Charge, it creates a rift that enables anyone to bridge the Cusps together to crossover to the neighbouring dimensions, but each of these Cusping Bridges has a time limit. Be wary that each rift would disappear in a matter of seconds so you have to pass through it as quickly as you can," he warned in advance, taking precautions to prevent any spacetime mishaps from happening to his new group of delvers. And to finish his set of instructions, he informed them that the Cuspmium crystals built into the Cuspers have a limited charge and should only be used if necessary.

They began to press the buttons, rifts began to form on the ground beneath their feet and they all fell through, travelling through the expanse of space and feeling their body disintegrate and reform, landing on the bushes below which cushioned their fall.

"Dale, could you please warn us about what these Cuspers are capable of before we use it? Like how it does its delving things?" Kadyn groaned in surprise, slightly irritated about Wendale's failure to give a forewarning.

"Sorry. I'm already used to this happening as a part of my routine, so I forgot about telling all of you rookie delvers this," he shrugged and answered, seeming blasé about the Cusp-crossing from Xenia, scratching his head in slight embarrassment.

Chapter 2

(Mysteries of Horizon)

When all the Empyreans were back up onto their feet, Wendale introduced them to the new world they were in, "Welcome to dimension 623, Horizon, the world of floating islands merely levitated by the psionic forces flowing around us. And just watch your step and don't fall into the void under the islands or you might never return, heh-heh," he chuckled under his breath facetiously while stating the dangers of their journey through Horizon. His words left the Empyreans to fret about moving around in that dimension, with the constant fear of slipping into the abyss.

Through his introduction to the dimension, he began vaguely recount the story when he last came a few years back, how Horizon was broken up into what they see now through a cataclysmic event, which he managed to avoid. Leaving some of the details aside for the last, he continued to talk about the reformed world as though he was a guide.

The more they followed their Cusper's Pathfinder, the more significantly the Empyreans could sense their powers diminish. Leo, who was the first to feel the brunt of the enervating effect, tried waving his arms around wildly to cast a spell, but nothing happened, appearing as though he was swatting flies.

The others, too, stopped in their movements to test out their powers. Ignis could not use her elemental magic and Kadyn felt that her body was weakened, unable to dash around at supersonic speeds like she normally could. However, both Kyudo and Seiche seemed physically unaffected, but they were able to feel the change.

"Dale, we can't use our powers around here. I can't even use my superspeed to check this place out in advance," Kadyn complained while she tested her powers by running about aimlessly. "What's the deal here?"

"One moment," he said as he rummaged through his backpack and took out a metallic disc, activating it as a holographic computer and started to initiate a proximity scan. As he moved his head closer to see its data, his eyes widened in realisation. "This makes so much sense now. It seems the psionic force has incongruous energy resonances reacting against the Empyrean magic. This dichotomy between the two impinges on the Empyrean magic by magnitudes which causes its diminishment, in turn rendering your Empyrean abilities useless."

"Uh… What?" The Empyreans uttered in unison about his incomprehensible scientific explanation, all confused by the amount of science thrown into their faces.

"So basically, your powers don't work due to the conflicting energies between the Empyrean and psionic forces here, in which they weaken your abilities and therefore, they're temporarily unusable while we're here."

After they knew had been going on from the point they set foot, they had no choice but to continue forward with their temporary afflictions. "According to the Pathfinder, the Cusp is located just two klicks away and it's relatively close to our current position," Wendale stated as they walked, leaping from island to island occasionally while they passed.

As they traversed the islands, they were silently concentrating on getting a correct footing for every step until they heard a gasp from Seiche, who had discovered a metallic staff stuck into the rocks which gleamed brightly in the sunlight and his eyes caught sight of it. Finding it queer that it was something out of the ordinary, he ran towards the staff and recognised that it was Asmodia's staff.

He knelt down and tugged the staff out of the rock. "I wonder how Asmodia's staff found its way here. I thought she dropped it on her home planet and was vaporized along with her in the explosion," he remarked as he passed it to Leo.

Leo inspected the staff and noticed that the words that had been etched into the staff was all weathered away but it was still slightly legible enough to read. "With the heavenly powers, the six Empyreans shall unite, lighting the darkness with unparalleled might." It was no doubt the words of the Empyrean Prophecy that Leo and the Empyreans fulfilled in the past before the staff was supposedly lost, along with Hades. This left him questioning in his mind, 'if Hades and the staff survived the explosion, that means Asmodia might still be out there somewhere too.'

He saved the thoughts of what could eventually happen for later, returning his concentration back to the cold metallic staff in hand.

As he held it, he could see that there was a thin coat of dust on the staff itself. He concluded that it had been left there, untouched for a considerable length of time. But while he held it for a longer period of time in his hands, he began having intense visions of Empyrea and the time he had with the other Empyreans in the past. Through the series of visions, he could hear Empyrea's voice faintly calling his name and had a look into the past, but before he could see any more, the visions stopped abruptly.

"I've just seen visions of the past, our past with Empyrea there with us. Why did Asmodia's staff allow me to see all these visions?"

"Actually, the staff was previously mine until Asmodia attacked Spiritus and stole it from me from my home planet. The worn engravings were the words of the Empyrean prophecy, were carved into the staff after I created it, to be fulfilled," Empyrea's voice echoed through their heads.

"Empyrea, where are you?"

"Leo, I'm essentially here. The staff contains parts of my power and therefore, my soul is linked to it, allowing me to speak to you through it as a medium. Before it was transported here, Asmodia formerly used it for her evil acts of raiding planets for resources and satisfaction, and when she was defeated, the words faded as the prophecy was fulfilled when all of you Empyreans vanquished her." There was a moment of silence before she continued, seeming to be hesitant as she spoke. "It's best if you leave the staff here and let the prophecy become evanescent, let it fade into the past and move on." Her words echoed into their heads and gradually became silent when she was finished.

With the staff in hand, he wedged it back into the rocks, leaving it as they found it and abandoning it forever as requested. Wendale and the Empyreans occasionally glanced back at the staff as it faded in the distance behind them until they could not see it anymore.

As the sky turned into a vermilion canvas with tinges of yellow and purple, they decided it would be best if they camped out like traditional explorers. Ignis suggested that she would start the campfire, but she quickly panicked when she remembered that her powers did not work on Horizon. Wendale, who had gadgets for almost everything, calmly whipped out a Xenian Igniter and kindled the gathered firewood with an acute discharge of plasma, before dexterously spinning it in his paws and plopped it back into his backpack.

With the fire started, they began to congregate around it and enjoy its warm embrace. While most of them were doing something else, Seiche began to roast marshmallows that he had brought along and started chomping them down afterwards. Kyudo, unlike him, silently watched the skies in wonder. "That's a nice sunset. It kinda reminds me of home, the warm orange glow persists before the night smothers it, the day resting in the peace of nightfall," he sighed as he watched the glow of the sun darken gradually, sitting in front of the smouldering fire, firewood crackling as it burned.

"Wow, *that's* deep," Kadyn commented in a slightly sarcastic tone, polishing her blade with a piece of cloth and some water, such that it would reflect the light of the fire.

"You know, Horizon was known for its picturesque, panoramic view of the sunrise and sunset, with beautiful colours that can be seen at and beyond the sky's horizon, hence its name," Wendale described as he laid back onto the grass behind him, his paws positioned under his head for support.

"That's a fitting name. No other name can make it sound more perfect," Ignis added, lying back alongside him, covering her long ears in the hood of her suit.

Leo sprawled beside them and enjoyed watching some of the constellations that he has not seen before, identifying the various shapes and symbols portrayed by the stars. With almost everyone laying on the ground to stargaze, Kadyn and Seiche soon followed along and they basked under the starlight of the skies as the crisp air blew past their faces once in a while.

They watched the skies deep into the night, having a nice view of the stars as they shifted slowly. Out of nowhere, they could see something move in the dark figure that hovered and lingered around directly above them. As they observed, it zoomed into the darkness, blending with the night sky and disappeared immediately.

"It's that thing again! That was what I saw during the few visits to Horizon that I've had over the years!" Wendale voiced out, recalling the times where he encountered or much less, sighted so close to him.

"But you don't know what that is, don't you?" Kadyn asked as she stared at the reflection in her scimitar, preparing to defend herself in case anything happens.

"Not a single clue till this day. That remains a mystery, even for the inhabitants. They call it the Shadow of Horizon, the mysterious black apparition that flies through the night every now and then."

Wendale finally revealed that this 'Shadow' was the one who wrought havoc onto Horizon, breaking the pristine solid ground of the world into the floating islands that they knew now. This got the Empyreans feeling slightly bothered about the fact that the 'Shadow' has the capability to blow up a planet and was currently looming above them.

When they asked why he did not tell them earlier, he shrugged and paused for a moment before explaining that he did not want to spoil the surprise for them. As they continued to guess who or what it was having some absurd ideas, they dozed off unknowingly as they carried on their conversations into the night.

When the next day arrived, they resumed their way towards the Cusp, only to discover that it was on an island that was floating above them. Without their powers or the appropriate equipment to ascend, they could not get up onto the island.

"Hmm... On occasion, the islands of Horizon align and misalign according to the seasons and timings. We've come at such an inopportune and it would be unreachable to us at this point, but, there might be a way," Wendale placed his paws at his chin as he thought deeply about the situation. As an idea popped into his mind, he snapped and suggested, "I shall bring you to meet an old friend of mine who might be able to help us out."

Chapter 3

(An Old Friend)

Wendale led them onto a different direction, crossing several islands until all they could see were rocky islands floating around them. On the island they were on, he meandered around the rocky outcrops and amidst the boulders revealed a rustic brick cottage with a roof constructed with bundled thatch.

As they got closer to the cottage, the door of the cottage was left slightly ajar and there appeared to be no sign of movement. Through the window, they could see a pair of curious eyes staring at them. Being respectful, they decided to wait outside the door until someone came and before long, the muffled banging of a hammer against metal could be heard from the inside.

"Brander, are you around?" Wendale called out after a few seconds. At the very same moment, the pair of eyes disappeared into the darkness of the cottage. He knocked on the door, awaiting a response and before long, a gust of wind blew in their faces as the door swung open with great force.

"Dale?" He turned to look at them as they approached, taken aback briefly before his face lit up with euphoria. With a swift swipe, he lifted Wendale up and hugged him with his massively built arms, squeezing him. In response, he wiggled his body around trying to break free as though he was like a squirming prey under the constriction of a snake. "Aye! What a sight fer sore eyes and surprise to see yer still in 'un piece, li'l Dale! I see yer brought yer friends too?"

"It's nice to see you after a decade!" Wendale stopped momentarily to catch his breath. "Empyreans, this is Brander, the Bovinean Blacksmith, and likewise. He's the one and only remaining in the entire world, crafting metallic tools for the inhabitants here to use."

"Aye, heh heh," Brander chuckled in pride as he scratched his head. "But li'l Dale, it's only been a couple of months since yer last came."

"Months? That can't be, right Dale?" Kadyn questioned his accuracy on information, finding it slightly peculiar. "What's going on here?"

"Hold your questions for a moment! Actually..." He used his paw to shift his spectacles upwards with a glint as it was raised. "This sort of time discrepancy would be the case of Spatio-temporal dilations occurring throughout the different dimensions in the realm of the Multiverse. In each world, the rate of time flows differently, as do the planets back in our dimensions, with day and night cycles at different speeds of time, quantifiable in ratios of minutes to days and so on. Does that make sense to you?"

"Uh-huh. Now, that makes *a lot of sense*," she replied, still uncertain of what just happened.

"It's a bit humid out 'ere. Why don't all of yer c'mon in fer some snacks? Some whiskey maybe? Let's chat fer a bit, shall we?" He dragged Wendale by his shoulder and invited them into his cottage, asking why they came to Horizon as he settled down on a wooden stool, sitting adjacent to his indoor workbench.

Wendale explained in short that they needed to travel to another place from Horizon as soon as possible, but without the right amenities to get to the unreachable floating island, they needed his help to get up there. Not wanting to trouble Brander too much, he requested for some hook and rope at the very least.

"Ropes wouldn't work fer all of ye. Some of ye would have problems, especially the scaley 'un there could really wear down the ropes," he laughed to himself followed by a short, awkward pause in his reasoning. "Unfortunately, fer now, I have nae, but I've got an idea of how to get ye all to yer destination. The li'l lass who lives with me might be able to help ye out." He suggested and turned his face in the direction of his workbench. "Faye?"

As they turned to where he looked at, they noticed a young white fox with several purple markings around her face, sidling around the workbench to get a better peek at them. She hid behind his workbench, standing with both her white paws held at the edge, her head slightly peering out from the side, afraid to get close to them.

"Forgive her. She's a wee bit shy. Ye see, Faye lost both her parents in one day when the destruction of Horizon happened. Not trusting anyone else, she came knockin' on the doors of me cottage 'un day as I knew her mother, seekin' refuge and care from me. Despite her loss, she was blessed with some powerful magic mojo that she'd occasionally use on me, heh-heh, somethin' to do with why the islands are floatin'. With that sort of stuff, I think she could get ye all up there without a hitch."

Faye added in her telepathic voice, "It's true. My powers are strong enough to bring you anywhere around here, even to that island where you need to go." She emerged slowly from the 'covers' of the workbench and held her tail close to her cheeks, still slightly bashful. "Please lead the way. I cannot locate where it is through my telepathy."

Wendale and the Empyreans felt a slight tingle in their heads as she spoke without any audible voice, just a unique feeling most of them felt for the first time. They were confused on how she managed to get into their minds so freely but decided not to think too much into it and began to lead her to where they wanted to go anyway.

While they walked towards the Cusp, Faye was busy telepathically talking to them as she floated in the air, recounting the story of how she lost her parents and the time she mastered her powers with the help of an unknown entity who talks to her in her sleep, soon becoming a precocious sorcerer of sorts in just the span of time she spent with Brander.

"Sounds like Empyrea to me," Ignis said, guessing that the entity could be her.

"I don't really who or what it was, so I couldn't tell its name either."

There was a bit of silence as they had to leap by several islands, concentrating on getting each step right, careful not to slip. It was, until Faye suddenly blurted out telepathically.

"Hey, I'm not some dumb kid, Kadyn. You feel useless without your powers and you're envious of me, am I right? I can read everything you're thinking," she 'said' with a cheeky smirk.

Kadyn's eyes shifted away from Faye and she blushed in embarrassment, indignant about being goaded and having her thoughts being read aloud. "Please stay out of my head," and following that came a stern warning in the form of a thought.

"Oops! I shouldn't have said it out loud," she apologized, placing both her paws at her snout in surprise and embarrassment upon realising her mistake. "But no more harassing me in your thoughts."

"Hmph!" She began to quicken her pace to avoid further embarrassment, trying to reduce the amount of time spent with Faye. Despite being slightly parted from her, she could still read Kadyn's mind where she saw all the alternative scenarios that could have played out if she had her powers, which were disturbing, even in her telepathic visions.

Reaching the floating island where the Cusp was, Faye raised her paws around creating a glowing outline around all of them, allowing them to float up to the island gradually with the bottomless void beneath their feet. When they set foot onto the island after a brief moment of flight, she bid goodbye telepathically as they thanked her and levitated herself back to Brander's cottage.

However, before they could activate their Cuspers to travel to the next world, they saw the Shadow once again, but this time in broad daylight, they could see him in more detail. He was draped in a Tyrian-purple robe etched with gold trimmings, his face hidden beneath the veils of the hood. As he turned towards them, he realised that he was being watched, his nightmarish red iris was somewhat off-putting and could be seen glaring creepily through the darkness of his hood. Bit by bit, he stepped backwards, seeming to retreat before he phased through a rift behind him.

The Empyreans turned to Wendale for an explanation, but in response, he shrugged, not knowing what it was from his experiences of dimensional travel. Without further delay, they pressed the buttons of the Cuspers and they zipped into the next dimension.

"Next up, one of my favourite dimensions, Dimension 624, Neoteric City, the city of revolutionary technology! Soon, all of you would enjoy the wonders there!" Wendale exclaimed in excitement as they passed through the cusping bridges transiting into the next world.

Chapter 4

(The Forsaken City)

As they left the bridging tunnel of the Cusp behind, they stepped onto a crosswalk of an empty metropolitan city, lifeless and silent as a deserted ghost town. Leaves, bits of paper and dust were blowing by in the howling wind as they stood where they were.

"Something's not right. When I first came here to Neoteric City, it was a bustling technological marvel of a city. Its people, the Neoterians, were utilising technology on par and beyond the advancements of Xenian-tech prevalently all around the streets, but now-" Wendale said dolefully before stopping, saddened by the sights that beheld his eyes. "Now, it's all abandoned and dysfunctional..."

After learning that the once lively city he loved was gone, he shuffled his feet despondently and sulked. As they strolled down the street, Ignis questioned out of curiosity why he was middle name was 'Mousse', additionally intending to steer his attention away from the desolate city to make him feel better.

He explained that on his home planet, there were different classes of mice people, the 'Mousses' being one of the upper-class races. "Also, anyone born in the 'Mousse' bloodline has much softer, whitish tufts of fur which feels like the creamy desserts, hence the origin of such a prestigious and elegant name."

While they continued their conversations on the way to the next Cusp, Seiche exclaimed, pointing at a wall, "it's him! It's that hooded devil of a shadow!" There was a poster plastered onto the wall with three big words, 'The Great Lezaros', the Shadow as they knew of previously, and several lines of information below the image of him.

"Hmm, the Great Lezaros?" Leo read out as he inspected the poster closer. "It says that he took over the leader of the city and ruled it for himself, and this poster was to gather the Neoterians to fight back. I guess it didn't turn out too well for everyone here once he found out the citizens turned on him."

"His face remains a mystery as long as he is hidden under that hood. I think I'll find out more about him while you guys saunter your way to the Cusp." Kadyn suggested. "Catch you slowpokes later once I'm done searching."

Straight away without hesitation, she zoomed off into the desolate cityscape and only occasional whooshing could be heard as she whizzed by them to move to another part of the city. After a bit of trawling through the city, she caught up to the group and returned with a holographic display panel which was surprisingly still intact.

"Apparently, this was the date he decided to wipe out every lifeform in the city," she stopped and raised the panel up, dimly displaying a picture showing the scene of a darkened city with the Great Lezaros launching balls of fire everywhere, showing one fireball heading in the direction of the panel, but the display switched off after a while. With a quick wave of elemental magic and an electrical zap from Ignis' paws, she started it up again and resumed showing the picture to everyone.

"Whoever who took this picture on this date had a last take just before they were burnt to a crisp. This Lezaros tyrant has no clear motive when he attacked the city at random the city but I believed he had something planned, like the last piece of the puzzle. Nevermind, I'm thinking too far ahead. Let's just move along and see what else we can find."

When they reached the Cusp's location, they were at the Technological Hub of the city, the building Wendale remembered entering countless of times during his inter-dimensional travels. He recounted that he had such a great deal of fascinating technology that it distracted him from his research and ran his time dry before he could ever move on to the next dimension every time he visited.

As they walked through the building's extensive ground floor area, they realized that their Cuspers detected three possible locations of the Cusp. It seemed peculiar to Wendale considering he has been through it on multiple occasions. Just to be sure that the Pathfinder function on their Cuspers were not just acting up, he decided to split the team up into three groups to locate these few Cusp coordinates.

He allocated the group into pairs, sending Ignis and Kadyn to search around on the ground floor, Seiche and Kyudo were to head towards the laboratory annexe, while he and Leo would go onto the roof where the Cusp has been located previously. "Any if any one finds the correct Cusp, please inform the rest through communication by Cuspers. Got it?"

They nodded in acknowledgement and split off into their pairs, using their Cuspers to find the definite location of the Cusp.

While moving about the ground floor to find the possible Cusp location, Kadyn realised that something was there at the other end of the ground floor and tapped on Ignis' shoulder, asking her to figure out what it was. They moved closer towards it and realised it was *him*. Kadyn stepped forward to confront him with both her scimitars unsheathed and crossed in front of her, preparing for an imminent brawl. Ignis took her stance behind her, already imagining how she was going to execute her powers.

"We know who you are, Lezaros, and you aren't *that* great. You are more of a coward, hiding under that hood!" she insulted aloud, attempting to intimidate him. "Reveal yourself!"

"My identity shall remain a mystery as long as I live. And, you don't really know who you're dealing with, do you?" He responded nonchalantly as he turned to face them, the whitish glint of his eyes were visible from the shroud of darkness concealing his face.

"I've been expecting you Empyreans to arrive as foreseen. Now, I'm going to eliminate all of you to make you learn who I really am!"

As he lunged himself towards them with both fists ready to punch them, Ignis whipped up a blizzard and blew him backwards with a flurry of ice, preventing him from contact onto Kadyn. However, he seemed unaffected, and in response, he waved his hands with the addition of a stronger blizzard, redirecting everything she threw back towards them. Ignis whipped up a wall of fire to defend herself while Kadyn persisted through his spell to attack.

Being resistant the extreme cold with her Empyrean abilities, she trudged through the winds of the blizzard using her blades to cover her face from the icy gusts and dashed in front pointing both her scimitars aimed towards Lezaros' neck at the very last moment. He evaded the sharp edge of her blades by a hair, following it up with another wave of his hand casting a sphere of electricity to discharge onto her body before she could reach him. This caused all the lights to flicker for a moment and impact of his spell sent her flying across the room.

When he stopped sending the blizzards towards them, Ignis bombarded him with bolts of ice and fire while she gradually stepped up closer and closer to him to finish him off. However, she was oblivious to the fact that it was just a duplicate projection of Lezaros until he teleported behind her and lobbed a slab of the building's wall at her, slamming her onto the ground with a cloud of dust and debris scattered all around her. As the wall's concrete shattered, he made the metallic rebar coil around her arms, pinning her down and immobilised her from making any additional movements.

"Don't try me. I, too, control the elements!" He said as he watched her struggle fruitlessly.

Seeing a short window of opportunity to strike, Kadyn stood up before she streaked speedily around him and to find the right time to finally land a hit on him, stirring the dust all around as she dashed around him.

"Try to catch me if you-"

Her words were cut-off the moment her taunt was interrupted by Lezaros' hand gripping around her neck tightly. "Don't play with me!"

With his fist full of immense dark magic, he threw her against the ceiling before another hit landed on her from behind, causing a great deal of pain when she landed back onto the floor. Lezaros left them in a great deal of agony and moved towards the annexe to take the second pair down.

Seiche and Kyudo nervously scanned the corners around the annex, searching the laboratory desks and equipment areas for the Cusp. While they were moving about, Kyudo noticed something from the corner of his eye - a faint black silhouette. As he turned to see what it was, it was gone.

"Whoa, somethin's flyin' around here! Lemme catch that nuisance!" Seiche announced as his eyes veered towards the black streak. With a rough estimate of where it trying to fly to, he utilized his scales and constructed a lasso, wrapping it around the flying object when it reappeared once more. As his scales coiled around the black object, they could hear a thud followed by a slight groan of pain.

They took a step closer to inspect who it was. To no surprise, it was Lezaros himself who was flying around them as a black shadow. In response to being caught, he freed himself easily with a wave of his hand, dispersing the scales back at Seiche. Responding hastily to the incoming projectiles, he used his scales to form a shield, deflecting the exploding scales and protecting both himself and Kyudo.

Using the shield in front of him as leverage, Kyudo leapt upwards in a somersault and landed behind Lezaros, firing a barrage of Empyrean energy arrows towards him while he flew through the air. However, his arrows seemed to disappear on the moment of contact with his body. As he tried to materialise different variants of arrows to shoot, it failed to cause any impact as they would somehow deflect off his body.

"You insolent fool!" Lezaros said as he walked towards Kyudo despite the countless arrows contacting him, dusting off his shoulder as if nothing happened. In desperation, he ceased his shots of arrows and fought him with his bow, but it was shortly ripped out of his hands and thrown aside. As the fight escalated, it had turned into a physical battle. Kyudo blocked and redirected every punch targeted at his body, focused on defending himself from the wrathful strikes of Lezaros' fists.

Seiche, on the other hand, stood beside in silence, aimlessly watching the fistfight as though it was entertainment. As Lezaros fought and parried, he pulled out a dirty trick out of nowhere. While Kyudo was distracted with one of his hands, his other charged up stealthily behind him. Before he knew it, Kyudo was hit with a gutful of magic, the intense surge of pain spreading throughout his body.

"Uh... I'm gonna go now," Seiche uttered under his breath tiptoed backwards in fear, trying to retreat from the brawl without getting harmed.

"You're next!" Lezaros turned towards him just as he talked to himself and charged at him and cast an intense wave of magic at him.

"Whoa whoa whoa! Whoa there!" Seiche exclaimed while he tried to promptly protect himself by formed a 'wall' out of his scales to block his attack. Unfortunately, his endeavours to alleviate the attack was futile against his great power, blasting through his 'wall' after an initial jolt and took him out as it perforated through his scaley construct. Once he was done with them, he teleported straight up to the roof, where the last pair were.

Meanwhile, Leo and Wendale, who had been unaware of the situation of the other pairs, continued to find the Cusp around the rooftops. They stepped through the tiled paths in the leading through the withering rooftop garden and probed around, scanning for any anomalies in energy signatures.

"Aha! I've managed to find the exact coordinates of the Cusp! I knew there could not be more than one Cusp existing at the same time. I'm gonna inform the rest!" He exclaimed excitedly. With a pause, he was ready to contact the rest. "Two and three, do you copy?"

However, his attempt to contact them was in vain as there was no response from them, only silence. This left both of them confused why no one had answered and stared at each other, speechless about what happened or what they could do.

Suddenly, Lezaros teleported behind them, startling them as they heard the sound of teleportation abruptly break the moment of silence. Wendale, being powerless and unable to deal with Lezaros, ran into the building for cover while Leo stayed to have a confrontation with him.

"The Great Lezaros, huh? I've been wanting to meet you." Instinctively, Leo charged up his hands with magic and turned to face Lezaros, preparing himself for a duel. As he began casting his spells towards him, Lezaros dodged his spells effortlessly and gradually moved closer, until they were staring face-to-face. Although his face was still hidden under his hood, the outline of his face could be seen with a grin.

"Do you think you could take me down? Even your friends have failed, so just give in to me!"

He waved his hands and immobilized Leo midair with dark magic, causing him to feel a strong crushing sensation under the spell, unable to retaliate. While still under the influence of the Lezaros' power, he was lifted over the edge of the roof, with an intention to throw him off. "No, this is too easy. I'll leave you for last. The next time we cross paths, you'll face oblivion and your friends, too, will suffer the *permanent* consequences if you try to stop me."

Once he was done, he waved his hands and flung Leo back towards the roof as if he was a doll. As he was thrown back onto the roof, he was liberated from the crushing spell but was too weak to move. He had a glimpse of him, watching him phase away through a rift while cackling balefully before he eventually passed out through exhaustion.

When Leo awoke from a hard slap to the face, he could see Wendale kneeling beside him with his paw above his head. Another slap his paw reached his face along with a nervous exclamation, "wake up, Leo! Please don't die!" Once he regained consciousness and popped his eyes wide open, he got slapped again, wincing at the pain of getting hit repeatedly, still stinging from the preceding few hits. "Dale! I'm awake! Please stop already!"

Acknowledging that Leo was finally awake, he stopped in his tracks after one more slap for confirmation that he was conscious.

"I'm so sorry, Leo. I thought that you were dead. I got worried for a second," Wendale shrugged before he picked up his items off the floor. "We must find the others. The Cuspers have a built-in tracking system so we should be able to find them fairly easily."

Pair by pair, they were found lying in torment. With the press of the shoulder portion of their suits, he activated the healing capabilities of the suit, healing their wounds rapidly while repairing the suit consecutively, allowing them to feel revitalised with everything restored to original condition.

After they shared about their different sides of the story from the experience they had with the Great Lezaros, Wendale decided it would be best to take precautions to avoid him as he could phase in and out of the dimensions easily by creating a rift, similar to the transdimensional capabilities of their Cuspers.

With all their wounds rapidly healed, they decided not to stick around any longer and agreed to move onwards in case Lezaros returned.

"By the way Leo, the next dimension is where the Empyrean life energy signature was detected. However, it's one of the dimensions I've never been to but read about in the past, a place which you might like and find familiar. Your friend Hades should be safe around there. Let's continue. Activate your Cuspers!"

With that, they were transported into a darkened world with black clouds overhanging like a huge blanket covering the light from the world, billowing in from all around them as they arrived.

Upon stepping on the grounds of the dimension, Leo was completely dumbfounded by the ruins surrounding them. There was a miasma of eeriness emanating from where they stood, but they could not figure out why they felt that way.

"So... Dimension 625, huh," Wendale, too, was also speechless. "This change wasn't described in the Multiverse Database..."

Chapter 5

(Home Sweet Home?)

"This is an alternate reality of Felineatius. I can recognise it anywhere by the unique shapes of these buildings, but this is nothing like my home where I'd live in," Leo stopped for a moment and checked his Cusper to see the time of the dimension and the Pathfinder. However, instead of seeing the time of the dimension, it displayed an "ERROR" message due to some sort of interference from all around. The Pathfinder was moving erratically, pointing at multiple directions at the same time, unable to seek out the Cusp, even the one they were close to.

Looking up at the sky, the sun was hung high up behind the clouds and Leo figured it was sometime in the late afternoon. He shared that at this time of the day when it was still bright, this path would have been bustling with Felineans, but there was not even a single trace of activity around, only dust blowing around like what they saw in Neoteric City. He guessed that it was another one of Lezaros' doings.

Wendale took out one of his intricately made contraptions and placed it on the ground, assembling itself into an antenna and sending an energy pulse through the air to detect any life forms. "Hmm, seems like this dimension is devoid of any lifeforms." There was a pause in his speech as he accessed the holographic display.

"Hold on a moment. I'm getting something. Yes... There seem to be one living being moving about in the Southern hemisphere."

As Leo observed the contours of the map, he recognised that the hills and valleys shown were somewhat familiar. "Hey, that's around my former neighbourhood. We could go there while we search for Hades," he exclaimed in excitement, giving him a chance to visit his alternate home.

Being a former inhabitant of Felineatius, Kadyn wanted to visit her alternate home too, but where she wanted to go was in the North. Leo was torn between the decision to find Hades and to go two ways to visit both their homes. He felt that sacrifices have to be made if they wanted any chance to find Hades alive. "Going North would be a long detour, which slows down the progress of our search down and isn't viable. There's no way we're travelling there if it's not convenient. But, we could always-"

"Y-You don't even think about I feel!" Kadyn interrupted him mid-sentence. "Being back home is what I dreamed of for years to come and you'd strike down my one dream just like that? You should *go south* then, just like your plans! I shall travel to towards the north on my own even if you're not coming along! Hmph!"

She stormed off into the distance, not even bothering to turn back to look at him.

"Kadyn?" Before he could even explain himself further, it was too late for his words to reach her for clarification. Leo sighed and sat on the remains of a wall with his head hung low, having thoughts on how he could have avoided the falling-out with Kadyn by phrasing his words correctly.

"Leo, Seiche and I will follow her from a distance to watch out for her and keep her safe. Don't worry about us. You should go find Hades," Kyudo suggested, pointing his bow towards where Kadyn went.

"Before we split up, this is the point where we'll regroup in a couple of weeks at most if need be. Be vigilant and contact each other through the Cuspers if you find anything. I'll follow Leo and Ignis towards the south," Wendale instructed, taking precaution just in case of any situation similar to what they experience in Neoteric City.

They walked in different directions and every time that they glanced back, their silhouettes gradually faded into the horizon until the two groups could not see each other. As the trio travelled, they passed through numerous ruins and debris of abandoned buildings, eventually reaching Leo's home after a three-day trip.

Outside his home, the sight of the ancient oak tree he used to hang around when he was younger dampened his spirit. It was charred and withered, and the swing that was once tied onto the tree was burned to a crisp, now a blackened block of wood with some length of rope still attached to its edges. Even in the alternate version of his home, while around these familiar places and buildings, he could still sense a certain sentimental connection to his cherished memories of his past before everything he had and knew were gone - the good days prior to Asmodia arrival.

To prevent any further delay in his schedule, he decided that he should move onwards and not brood over his past. He pressed onwards to his alternate home, which had been partially destroyed with most walls still intact, unlike the rest of the buildings around that were a wreck. Stepping into his home was a nostalgic experience to him as he began reminiscing about the times he had using some of the odds and ends around the house, be it its position or its current condition as he picked up and placed down one after another to examine. While the rest looked through the nooks and crannies of the first floor, he climbed up the flight of stairs to where his room used to be and trawled around.

Shifting the remains of furniture around to clear the path into his room, Leo discovered the Empyrean Shard lying on the dusty floor. As he picked it up, he felt that it was cold, unlike the Shard he had in his possession formally, this Shard was neither luminous nor warm, seemingly sapped of its Empyrean energies. He left it back at where he had found it and stepped out onto the stargazing balcony.

At the balcony, he discovered his family's heirloom, one that was passed down through his family to him. It was the Stargazers' telescope, surprisingly still in workable condition after brushing the thick layers of dust off the lens. The sun was setting in the horizon like a ball of orange melting into the blue backdrops of the skies, transitioning into the inky darkness, the only time when he could view stars through his telescope clearly. In the midst of scanning the skies through the lens of the telescope, Ignis brought him a tattered Xenian Date calendar with dates of several months crossed out. Wendale, following closely behind Ignis, requested that Leo tried to determine the dates using the stars as he was well-versed with astronomy, so that they could gauge how far into the future Alternate Felineatius was.

He used the telescope to view the azimuth of the stars, each dot in the sky giving pieces of information from each position to finally fit everything together as a complete puzzle to calculate the exact date there. The date he determined was the date was a few decades after the day the planet was supposedly destroyed. He was mystified about how Felineatius was still in one piece. After a moment of thought, he decided to resume their search for Hades and leave the thinking for later.

As they closed in towards the coordinates where Empyrean life signatures have been detected, possibly Hades, Leo began to feel that the atmosphere has gone slightly awry. After all the clues and discoveries that he made, he knew that something was off. He looked back at his Cusper and gasped as his intuition was right. The Cusper started picking up multiple Empyrean energy signatures of lifeforms popping out of nowhere. Wendale and Ignis, too, stared blankly at their Cuspers, unable to comprehend the mess they have gotten into. Strange pulsating rifts started to appear all around and Wendale shouted out anxiously, "Those are dimensional anomalies! Don't touch them! Run and don't stop no matter what!"

They ran as quickly as they could and managed to avoid the anomalies on their way to the nearest shelter they could find, Leo's house. While they dashed towards the house, they attempted to contact the rest, but what they could only hear was Seiche's voice. "Leo... BZZZT... We're surrounded by... BZZZT... Kadyn was sucked down some glowin' dimensional whirlpool of sorts and so was Kyudo. I'm still... BZZZT... It's under me! Ah!" After his last exclamation, all they could hear was static. They slowed down to a halt for a moment to check the trio's Cusper locations using the Pathfinder.

"They're gone... We have to leave this dimension as soon as possible and return back to Xenia without them. This dimension isn't stable. Those anomalies could transport you anywhere in the Multiverse, even beyond the Cuspers' reach," Wendale stated reluctantly, still slightly breathless from running. "However, one thing that I discovered about the anomalies is that they have energy signatures similar to that of an Empyrean's which is quite unusual for such an anomaly. These kinds of discoveries might be..."

"Hold on, Dale," Leo interjected as he got distracted by a familiar outline in the distance. "Is that Hades?"

Without any consideration of the risks and his strong emotional urge to reunite with Hades clouding his thoughts, he darted towards what he thought to be him, screaming his name in joy after being separated from him for so long. But what he saw was not him, but a deceiving mirage from afar. By the time he realised what it was, an anomalous rift tore open through the ground in front of him, pulling him into it.

"Leo!" Wendale and Ignis rushed to his aid and attempted to pull him out by his arm, fighting against the forces of the anomaly. It was still not enough and the anomaly dragged all of them through a long iridescent spatial tunnel, transporting them into a far-off part of the Multiverse while they fell.

Chapter 6

(Stranded)

Once they dropped out of the spatial tunnel, they fell into a forest where the air was crisp and invigorating. The trio viewed their Cusper holograms simultaneously for the number for the dimension they were on and they stared blankly at each other. Examining the area around them, they were greeted by the sight of Seiche running in their direction waving at them in excitement while Kyudo calmly followed along behind, walking towards them.

"Hey, ya three!" Seiche exclaimed in an explosive manner such that it caused them to briefly jump out of their skins. "It's great and all that you're fine, but, as you can see, Kadyn isn't with us. I don't know where in the world she'd washed-up, but she's somewhere in the sea of the Multiverse." They were speechless for a few seconds as they became aware of her absence.

"So, where are we on the dimensional charts, Dale?"

"Unfortunately for us, Seiche... We're in Dimension 391, far from the comforts of home. Furthermore, the used Cuspmium crystals in the Cuspers doesn't have the charge to bring us back to Xenia through that many dimensions. I didn't replace the partially-used crystals, thinking that we wouldn't go this far. We're stuck here now, because of me..." Wendale's ears drooped and his head hung low, thinking that he was to blame for their predicament.

"Don't worry, Dale. This is just a bump in the road. If we're stuck here, we might as well check out what's in store for us. Maybe we'll like it here," Ignis affirmed. "Let's find the good opportunities in this turn of events."

"Yeah! We should go with the flow, dudes. If we were to force ourselves through, it might turn out worse, maybe an existential wipeout from the Multiverse."

"Seiche, hush! Don't jinx it!" Ignis smacked him lightly on his head with her paw.

"Ow… Alright, alright."

While the rest began setting off, Wendale stared at his screen, distracted by the screens of data he had on his holographic disc. "It seems that the dimension we're in currently has some traces of energy which has the same resonance as your…"

He looked up from the screens, only to see them in the distance already walking away.

"H-hey! Wait up, Empyreans!" He shouted, running to catch up to them.

They began their trek through the nearby underbrush, approaching a clearing which was an idyllic, flower-filled meadow with diversities and vibrant colours of the flowers. When they walked through the meadow, Ignis began vigorously sniffing the air around her. "Something feels familiar around here but I think it's just a hunch."

"Yeah. Come to think of it, the scent and colours remind me of your cabin back on Elementus where you lived before you moved to Xenia, I wouldn't question anything if this was where you came from. We just might never know," Leo added, recollecting the day when both he and Hades first found her on wandering about the highlands of Elementus while they were on the quest to find all the other Empyreans.

"Hmm…" Upon hearing what he said, Ignis pondered deeper into thought on how she got acquainted with the scents of those flowers. "Well, I planted those flowers around my cabin from the seeds given as a parting gift by my foster before I moved up there. But it seems as though those seeds came from here…" She continued to ramble on and gradually got lost in her imaginative thoughts, clasping her paws together and thinking of what a wonderful life if she had lived with her parents here.

By the time they crossed the meadow to the forest on the other side, they were exhausted from the long journey under the sultry weather and decided they needed a break before they continued. While they moved through the forest, Ignis heard the thundering sounds of a hidden waterfall originating from behind a big boulder with her highly-sensitive ears. She exclaimed excitedly to the rest that they could relax and wash up there from the journey to continue a bit later. Despite being doubtful that there was really a waterfall, they decided to follow her, hoping to wash up and find some rest.

As they passed the big boulder, it opened up into a quarry with a crashing waterfall, the running waters were frothing with bubbles. The waters below the waterfall crystal clear, seeming pristine until now. They swiftly unpacked and dove straight into the welcoming waters to cool off and finally relax before continuing their journey forward. Kyudo, the only one who did not jump in immediately, went off into the woods to scour the forest for some firewood and twigs to boil his tea, slinging his ornate bow around his chest to arm himself in case anything happened.

While in the water, they began doing their own activities. Ignis formed up an icy cup and floating chair with her elemental magic, and whipped out a bottle of fruit punch she had brought along for the delve. After a few steps of preparation, she 'voyaged' through the waters on her icy throne and sipped away the cold tangy juice with a pair of icy shades.

Wendale, unlike the trio who immersed themselves completely, decided to just soak his feet in the waters, not wanting to get himself wet for the trouble of drying himself off later. Leo and Seiche, however, begun to splash each other, gradually increasing the vigour of their splashes. Soon, Ignis eventually hopped off her "throne" and joined in, splashing each other to both have the satisfaction of sending water into someone's face while being refreshed by the cool, incoming water.

To top everything off, Seiche stepped out of the water, grappled up to the top of the waterfall using a rope constructed from his scales and formed a surfboard. Following that, he surfed down the vertical wall of water, causing an enormous splash upon reaching the bottom, with the wave of the impact washing everyone who was in the water and ashore. There was a moment of astonishment and silence as they stared at Wendale's who was now wet before everyone burst into laughter. And, a wave of realisation hit Leo as the peals of laughter died down.

"It's a really long time for Kyudo to gather firewood. Usually, he's speedy and efficient in terms of collecting them. Something is amiss about it..." Leo put his hand on his chin and thought.

"Um, dudes? The Lezaros creep is back. I'm gonna get him this time!" His train of thought was abruptly broken by Seiche's sudden exclamation, pointing at *him* on the edge of the waterfall where *he* was standing.

Without thinking, he grappled up the waterfall and got himself in hot pursuit, catching all of the rest off guard as he abruptly swung up in a split second through the air. The others followed closely behind up to the top, but they were stopped in their tracks when an arrow was shot in front of them. They around but no one was there, not even Seiche. As they moved another step, another arrow came from the sky, landing right in front of Wendale.

"Ah! What's this?" He exclaimed, stepping backwards in astonishment.

"Could that be Kyudo's arrow?" Ignis questioned as she knelt down to observe it closer.

"It couldn't be. From the looks of it, these arrows appear to differ from the shapes and sizes of what he uses," Leo said as he picked up the arrow and examined it closely, specifically on detail. He explained that Kyudo would usually go for heavier metallic arrows while the one he held was light, feather-fletched and its arrowhead and shaft carved purely from wood. He concluded that it was most likely to miss its targets in windy conditions, like the one they were experiencing at the moment, and not one of Kyudo's.

"Looks like you know your teammates well, Leo."

"Well, Dale, you see..." Leo began scratching his head. "It's best to know your friends and their weaknesses, especially if we're working together."

Just as he tossed the arrow back onto the ground, a whole barrage of arrows was sent heading in their direction from the sky. Instinctively without hesitation, Leo used his Empyrean magic to form a forcefield, deflecting all the arrows from hitting them. When the arrows stopped raining from the air, several heavily armoured knights approached them with various metallic weapons, and their face was hidden under the medieval visors that they wore.

"Come with us, or else..." One of them demanded, pointing a silvery sword towards them.

"Or else, what?" Ignis asked teasingly with her arms akimbo and her head leaned forward, interrupting his train of thought.

"We'll think of something later. Now, come with us and you'll not be harmed! Hmph!" He shouted, slightly aggravated by her mischief.

The next moment, they could hear some of the other knights whisper "no promises though" followed by a soft snicker which resounded through their metallic headpiece.

They were escorted past the hill and behind it was a white stone castle rampart overspread with vines. As the massive drawbridge lowered with the sonorous creaking of the huge metallic hinges and cacophony of the chains clanking against each other. The knights shoved them every now and then into the castle, taking them up the castle into an enormous throne room. Upon entering the chamber, Ignis' face lit up as she knew her intuition was right about where they were - she was home.

Chapter 7

(The Sylvian Kingdom)

On the throne sat the Queen, a svelte Sylvian Hare with long flowing blonde hair, her fur of a tanned-brown hue and she had a jewel-embellished royal sceptre in her right paw. She was admiring the shimmering of the gems on her sceptre, right before they barged in.

"Your Majesty, these are some more of the brainwashed enemy outsiders we have found wandering about the fields. What should we do with them?" the leader of the knights asked her, leaving her to decide their fate.

"They don't look like the normal ones who would attack us. But just to be sure, take them away for the time being and put them on trial," she instructed her retinue along with the gesture of her sceptre, without even a single look at them.

"Wait no, no, no! We're not brainwashed! Please-"

"That's what a brainwashed soldier would say. Move it!" Ignis' plea was cut short by the knight pushing her away.

While the trio was being relocated again, the Queen suddenly voiced out, "hold on a moment. I know that specific thumping of a Sylvian's foot anywhere, that particular soft and muffled tap on the ground," she stopped them in their movements, confirming her guess as she raised her head and sighted a Sylvian within the group. She shifted her gaze towards Ignis, intently observing from her throne.

"Your thumping rhythm suggests that you're from the kingdom, but..." Rubbing her eyes with her paws to ensure that she was not seeing things, what she was looking at was a mirror image of herself, from the certain distinct facial features to outward appearances. "Might I ask, where do you hail from, young Sylvian?"

"I was taken in by a foster as an infant by an elemental of the Elementus, tasked by Empyrea to protect me from any danger, and..."

"Empyrea? Now, where have I heard the name before?" the Queen murmured to herself just as the name was mentioned, still listening in detail to what she had to say.

She continued to relate the story of how she went with the Empyreans to fulfil the prophecy until the Queen interrupted her as she realised at the point in time why her name was so familiar.

"I can't believe it. You're my daughter! A few years back, I sent you away to protect you with the sworn promise by Empyrea that you'll return, and now you've finally returned home!" In a few swift gesticulations, all the knights knew what she wanted and left the throne room immediately for some privacy, leaving two knights to guard the entrance.

Leo, who heard the Queen speak about Empyrea, was keen on asking her more about it but kept his question until it was the appropriate time. After the guards left them, she stood up from her throne. Step by step, she walked gracefully towards them. "I'm sorry about whatever that happened. I didn't expect guests to come by my kingdom, especially after the recent attacks. I am Queen Sophia of the Western Sylvian Kingdom, the last kingdom left standing."

They had a round of introductions before she stepped closer to Ignis and inspected her scrupulously from top to bottom, tugging gently at the sleeves as she observed. "What are you doing in such strange clothes, young lady?"

"Well, your Majesty... We travelled from far away and had to get here through different sorts of places, so we needed to be readily prepared for anything. And these suits protect us from different environments and provide real-time translations to different native languages and so on."

"And, even with all those preparation, I'm sure you aren't prepared for a feast?" she asked and soon after, everyone around the throne room had a hearty laughter.

"It's great to be back with you, mum!" Ignis hugged her, with one of her feet raised in the air behind her in happiness. In response, she hugged her back for a while and caressed her hair, looking at her eye to eye, remarking on how beautiful she had become after all those years. "I'll get you ready for tonight."

Signalling once more with her paws, the remaining royal subjects in the room began to move about hastily in preparation for the feast. Afterwards, she whispered into one of the knight's ears and he hastily stepped out of the throne room.

"Before we move to the dining hall, do you know this rowdy lady that we've captured earlier this week?" she questioned, as soon as the knights brought Kadyn into the throne room. Ignis nodded and told her about Kadyn and convince her that she was with them and therefore, not an enemy, requesting the Queen to set her free.

When she was freed, both she and Leo gazed at each other in silence before he apologized about what happened back on Alternate Felineatius, not being able to explain himself properly until now. For a moment she hesitated before forgiving him, letting their bygones be bygones.

"I guess that's what I get for being too quickly riled up and rash on you," she nudged Leo. "But!" She held up one finger, "being in this Sylvian world is the worst. You'll know why during the *feast*," she warned with air quotes while they ambled their way towards the dining hall.

Behind their backs, Ignis nudged Wendale on his arm and began to whisper. "Arguing, it's what couples do, am I right?"

"Tell me about it!" Both of them tittered about it, not wanting them to overhear their laughter.

With the assistance from the royal helpers who brought her into the upper levels of the castle, Ignis was spruced up in a sleek, royal silk dress for the feast. After a lap of preparation for the rest, they were all escorted into a grand dining hall with a long table regaled with food, but unlike normal feasts, the one colour they could see predominantly was orange. While the rest picked random seats around the table, Ignis bobbed a curtsy in her dress before settling down on the opposite end of Queen Sophia's seat, nervously awaiting her signal to initiate the feast.

The chefs started their lively dances around the table while the musicians played their violins, reading the list of all the dishes that they had on the table in a little jingle. As they continued, they began to pour juice into their silver chalices from a height, smoothly raining down the orange-hued liquids as if it was a long flowing river. With all the chalices filled, the Queen gave the signal to begin.

At one glance, they were deluged by the available options they were presented with. Unlike the rest, Kadyn had a look of disgust on her face and started to fidget with her cutlery, namely, her knife, flicking it front to back and so on. From time to time, Ignis was constantly chivvying her not to fiddle with the cutlery to prevent her from embarrassment, although each reminder failed to get it through her head.

"C'mon, Kadyn. Why are you still waffling over what to eat? All of these look scrumptious to me," Ignis whispered softly to him.

"Well, first of all, you're a Sylvian and second, it's not that I don't know what I want to eat, but I'm a little sick of eating carrots all day, which was all they gave in the prisons. I had to force myself to swallow them for survival," she whispered back, slightly jaded about eating more food made of carrots.

"True, and I thought that there'd be *at least* a dish of meat in a royal feast," Wendale added in a flippant tone.

Unfortunately, while both of them were grumbling silently to Ignis, they were oblivious that their whispers echoed throughout the dining hall and could be heard from across the table to the other side of the table by the sensitive ears of the Sylvians.

"What did you just say?" Queen Sophia questioned them from her end, catching the attention of the others.

Wendale swallowed hard as the dining hall turned silent, his tail between her legs from his complaints being heard. Kadyn did not react as dramatically as him physically but internally, she felt a certain bit of uneasiness. The rest were tensed up with anxiety painted over their faces, fearing that the Queen would mete-out harsh punishments on them.

Ignis shifted her eyes to cue Wendale to apologize first, but before he ever had the chance to open his mouth, Queen Sophia spoke, "We, the Sylvian people, originate from herbivorous roots and will not take meat for a meal, if it means culling for food." She paused for a moment, seeing every one of the guests, especially Wendale, breaking out in cold sweat.

Being her guests for the first time, she reassured the two that she would let this incident pass as a one-off event because they were not used to their culture and customs, stating that subsequent times would be counted as treason. They heaved a sigh of relief as the tension ceased, but they still felt a sense of discomfort as other Sylvians shifted their eyes towards them every once in a while.

When everything was moving smoothly again, Leo decided that it was the right time to question Queen Sophia how she got to know about Empyrea.

She retold the story, the tale before their lands flourished, when it was just a barren landscape. The Sylvians had to struggle to grow their main source of food - carrots. It was not until Empyrea showed herself and brought her ancestors an ample source of nourishment by turning their infertile land into the very soil that they have to this day. Soon, they could grow enough to eat and survive and they became her followers and were eternally grateful for what she had done for the Sylvians.

Ignis brought up another question about why she thought that they were 'enemies' earlier.

She explained the whole situation that someone in a purple cloak by the name of the 'Great Lezaros' came from a glowing hole and invaded the other kingdoms, his seething hatred ensued from the Sylvians' beliefs that Empyrea was their messiah.

Even fighting alone, he was strong enough to control even the minds and bodies of the Sylvians to do his bidding, being seen as a big threat to everyone. Being fearful that he might one day attack her kingdom with the brainwashed Sylvians from the other kingdoms, she sent Ignis away with Empyrea to safeguard her.

After she had been sent away, Lezaros attacked the Eastern kingdom and many of the survivors flocked to her kingdom, the last in line to be dominated by him. Subsequently, he tried to attack her kingdom in the past few years.

She then turned to look at Ignis, her eyes were slightly tearing up. "In desperation, King Nero, your father, went up against Lezaros but he was taken by storm, an ambush which silenced him, long before he could strike. Even now, I fear an all-out attack to the kingdom is imminent and the wrath of Lezaros is forthcoming. And as the storm of darkness brews close, the end of the Sylvians encroaches upon us."

"You mean like that?" Seiche pointed through the arrow slits in the walls of the dining hall, a literal storm was rolling in as she spoke of it. "It does look like a stormy day to me!"

She turned to have a look at what he saw and gasped, horrified that the invasion was actually happening at the very moment. Gusts of wind could be heard howling through the arrow slits. Blaring intermittent beeping could be heard emanating from Wendale's backpack. As he dug through his backpack for the source of the sounds, he discovered that it was his Empyrean Detector on his Cusper that was glowing red, insinuating that Lezaros was coming. It indicated that the Empyrean energy signatures detected had gone off the scale and was still rising. With his face buried in the Cusper's hologram, he was oblivious that the rest had left the room.

"Um, Empyreans? I have something to tell you about the-" before he could share this information with them, he realised that they had already gone to prepare for the invasion. He sighed and grumbled to himself as he watched from the arrow slit, "some heroes just don't care about sciencey stuff…" Shaking his head, he searched for a safe spot he could hide in the castle for the time being to distance himself from the fray.

With all their gear and weapons readily equipped, the Empyreans stood in frontlines of the kingdom and were anticipating Lezaros' imminent attack. The Sylvian army, however, was fearful for more losses and only the Sylvian bowmen stayed on the ramparts of the castle, equipped with fire arrows while the rest hid under the safeguard of the castle walls.

Queen Sophia stood and watched from afar, dressed in a metallic suit of armour while wielding a silvery sword adorned with jewels and carved runic inscriptions on the blade of her sword.

"Steel yourselves, Empyreans and fellow Sylvians! He's coming!" She voiced out from the balcony of the castle, pointing her sword toward where the groups were headed to.

Chapter 8

(The Great Revelation)

In the darkened, foreboding skies, the black clouds rolled in with dark red and purple hues, followed by a final ominous purple flash lit the clouds ablaze. Amidst the lights came a thunderous bellowing followed instantly by a purplish streak, slamming onto the ground with great force, forming a crater in the wake of his heavy impact. It was *him*.

"I've been waiting for you to arrive right into my trap, Empyreans," he stopped for a while, standing back up from his crouched landing position. "For me to end all of you in one fell swoop."

"Well, it seems by coincidence, we've all come to stop you, Lezaros. It ends here," Kadyn responded aggressively as the Empyreans inched their way closer to him, armed and pumped up for the fight.

"It's a bit unfair don't you think, with the Empyreans and the army all against me?" he snapped his fingers and brought time to a halt, stopping Kadyn midair with her scimitars ready to strike at any moment, leaving only Leo to fend for himself, as he was immune to the stoppage of time with his Empyrean abilities. "Let's take this one on one and get this over with, shall we?" He raised his left hand and clenched it into a fist, causing all of the Empyreans and Sylvian bowmen to collapse instantaneously as if they were marionettes with their strings cut.

The launched himself upward in a huge burst of magic and opened up a rift in front of him as he flew off. Leo gave chase to Lezaros, flying through the rift to catch up with him, but he was oblivious that going through the rifts were detrimental to his Cuspmium charges. Lezaros knew about his Cusper at first glance and was intentionally using up the charges on his Cusper. Being unable to travel through dimensions as he did, Leo was dependent on the Cusper to travel through worlds to prevent the dimensional strain on his body.

When he finally stopped, they were in Alternate Felineatius. As he stepped into the dimension, his Cusper started beeping and he checked it immediately. Unfortunately, it was almost de-energized of its charges from travelling through over a hundred dimensions so quickly, with only a few charges left to spare for getting back to Xenia.

"Stop playing games with me! No more running!"

Leo flew towards him sending bluish bolts of magic in his direction, but each one had been deflected off his body as if he was automatically shielded. In retaliation, he fought back with crimson spheres of magic, just like the colour of darkness that he had welled up in his heart used as a fuel for his magical strength. While they exchanged their blows of magic, Lezaros began to intensify his spells, sending a massive wave of magic at him.

Despite casting a magical shield in front of him, he was unable to defend himself against the sudden surge in power and was tossed through walls into one of the buildings. Before he could get up to face him, he felt Lezaros' magic restraint his body. However, this time he could sense that something was 'Empyrean' with his magic, a familiar tingling sensation that reminded him of the time he felt his powers develop on the first touch of the Shard.

With another blast, Leo was sent ramming through the ruins into the alternate Leo's home. He let out a few groans from the affliction to his body but managed to get up from the ground to face Lezaros.

"I know who you are, Lezaros," Leo sputtered out while trying to catch his breath after putting the bits of clues together. "You are me, aren't you? An alternate Leo Stargazer from this dimension, just that you strayed off the path of good."

"Well-well-well, you've finally figured out. I was the Empyrean signature that your friend detected, a red herring to lure me into my trap while throwing you off course from your search," Lezaros slowly removed his hood, revealing his face as an alternate version of Leo, but instead, his fur was white and his hair was unkempt. He had a slash scar across his left cheek and a sinistrous grin scribbled on his face. Instinctively, Leo knew he was a tough adversary as the villains with scars were no mean feat to subdue from his experience defending Xenia from invaders. His visage revealed everything from his first impressions without the need for guesses that those were the signs of his violent past. "That, along with my greatest plan to eliminate you once and for all!"

Giving no time for him to breath, he dragged Leo up into the air and almost immediately, continued to exchange their blows of magic at each other, destroying the ruins around them in the process. With massive forces of spells missing each other by the hair, Lezaros stepped it up a bit and opened up another rift to another dimension, fleeing from the battle midway with a devilish plan in mind.

As Leo sighted him phasing away into another dimension, he prepared to travel himself, but there was one, unsettled problem. 'This is the last charge of my Cusper. Once I'm through the rift, I'll be stuck there forever.' He thought to himself while trying to decide whether he wanted to pursue him. With his choice in mind, he decided to follow closely behind, using his remaining Cusper charges to travel through the rift. On the other side, he realised that he was on the crosswalk of Neoteric City, the one he passed through before.

"Ah... Neoteric City, the first of the dimensions I've ever ruled and enslaved. Once a city of innovation and marvels, not anymore when they tried to overthrow me. Even with the help of their technological weapon, their powers were vapid and meaningless compared to mine."

His limbs were gripped with Lezaros' power once more and lifted into the air, feeling the Cusper on his right arm shaking vigorously.

"You're pathetic. You can't even fully control the powers of time and space, requiring the aid of Neoterian technology to pass through dimensions." He removed the Cusper from his wrist and pulverised it into dust in an instant with his powers. Still immobilised in the air, he was unable to protest or retaliate.

"Needless to say, I've been watching you as you grow through the dimensional Multiverse, unable to unleash your full power without an external trigger. Unlike you, I've gained unlimited power by draining the energies from the Empyrean Shard. With all these power coursing through my veins, I could feel the impulse to do even more and sought to be the dominant one of time and space, expanding the extent of my powers across countless worlds."

"Greed begets more greed, Lezaros. You can never be satisfied!"

"On the contrary," he denied, holding Leo's face by the chin and forcing him to look eye to eye. "My lust for dominance was satiated by the voices of my victims' pleas, cries, and finally, silence. Anyone who stood in my way, I'll have the pleasure of rooting them out and obliterating them. You're the hardest to eliminate of them all!"

Lezaros dragged Leo by his collar and forcefully transported him through the rift, releasing his grasp on the other side, thrown onto the grounds of one of the floating islands of Horizon. Being forced through the Cusp without his Cusper, he felt weaker, gradually turning frail from the dimensional forces acting on him, straining on his physical body close to its limits.

'This isn't good,' Leo thought as he flew back up to where Lezaros was.

"I intended to destroy this world completely with my powers, but instead reshaped this world into an anti-Empyrean one, so any kind of Empyrean energy will slowly seep away, and eventually, this shall become your grave. With the alternative dark magic I have in my grasp, I'm unaffected by the forces whereas you'll be powerless in a matter of seconds. There's no escape for you now as my plan unfolds, not even with your soul when I drop you down into the void."

He felt progressively enervated while they continued their onslaught on each other and the intensity of his spells began to falter as his powers conflicted with the surrounding force, the diminishment of his physical strength became apparent as well. And soon, he began running out of steam to fight, Lezaros sent a last jolt of magic towards his gut, hurling him up into the air before another blitz of magic threw him back down onto the ground.

Leo sprawled on the ground with agony searing through his body and he felt his vitality beginning to wane. With another few more hard impacts, the pain took its toll on his body, leaving him with a numbing sensation jarring throughout his body, turning colder has his body began to give in.

He stared at Lezaros above him, his body surged with powers and his body was shrouded in a bright, crimson aura. His fur seemed to appear as if it was on fire and a crimson glow was emanating from his eyes. Shifting both his hands together, he was charging up a concentrated sphere of reddish magic, preparing for his execution. Life flashed before his eyes as the charging ball grew bigger and brighter. He closed his eyes and anticipated the end of his journey as defeating Lezaros was too obstinate of a task for him with the odds stacked against him.

"It's the end of the line for you, Leo," he said with a grin, and with a thrust of his hand, he sent the immense sphere of dark magic and the air around vibrated as it headed straight for him.

Just as he was on the verge of giving up, he could feel the ceasing of time and space, a cosmic stoppage that even Lezaros could not interrupt with his abilities. In the temporal pause, he could hear Empyrea's voice. "It's not the end. Leo, your sources of powers are not limited. Even the psionic forces of Horizon can be altered for your personal Empyrean charge, where your powers are normally diminished. But, altering this kind of power will intensify your own tenfold which might entail corruption if not careful, like how Lezaros succumbed to the clutches of darkness as he was controlled by unknown powers, unable to take control of them. Make it right, Leo, and cleanse his corruption with the touch of his heart."

As space and time unfroze again, Leo was slightly confused about Empyrea's words but he could feel his body upsurging with the energies drawn from all around. He was endowed with adequate power to reach his peak in spite of the conditions of Horizon, flaring up with a blinding burst of light into his ultimate form - the Light of the Empyreans. At his culmination of power, his body started overflowing with intense magic after his Empyrean energies became one with Horizon's Force. It was time to turn the tables on Lezaros.

Hastily, before the hurtling sphere could hit him, he veered away from it and dodged it by a whisker, only feeling the strong vibrations caused by the forceful impact afterwards running down his spine and tailbone. With the elevated powers that he had currently, he flew up into the air, staring Lezaros face to face and tried opening up a rift behind him.

As the air tore open into a rift, Leo was internally surprised for a split second about actually doing it before he darted towards Lezaros and pushed him through, continuing exchanging flurries of intense magic at each other, chasing him through different dimensional landscapes.

In each transition from dimension to dimension, Leo landed a few spells onto Lezaros as he tried to flee, debilitating him one peg at a time by wearing his power out using the features unique environments of each world to his advantage. As time went on, Lezaros' attempts to fight back were futile and resulted in him getting hit by Leo's spells more often.

When they finally returned to the Sylvian kingdom, Leo sent a blast of magic onto Lezaros' back which resulted in causing him to crash onto the ground. With no stamina left to retaliate, he laid on the ground facing upwards gasping for his breath, he conceded in defeat to Leo and awaited the final blow to end him.

"Do it! You know what comes next," Lezaros closed his eyes with a taut grin as he leaned his head onto the ground.

"No. There must be another way... I know there's still good in you somewhere."

Chapter 9

(Making It Right)

'Cleanse his corruption with the touch of his heart,' Empyrea's words sprang into his mind, reverberating around his head. With her message deciphered, Leo dived down towards him and sent a pulse of Empyrean energy through Lezaros' heart. Viewing his memory through his energy, what Leo saw was a darker path with bloodshed, his past was changed to his favour and he became greedy, tracking down all the other Empyreans for their power, except Empyrea who seemed to evade his every attempt to eliminate her.

Leo decided it was best to share his past memories and lessons learned throughout the years from both sides while allowing him to understand the true purpose of his Empyrean powers, and eventually taught him the correct path into the future.

"All this while, you have abused your power for evil and greed through committing sacrilege, but there will always be light in the darkness, never to be snuffed out, even if your past was dreadful. It is up to you whether you embrace the light in the despairing plights of the past and find opportunities to make things right in the future, or fall victim into the dark abyss that you cannot get out of. The past cannot push you down, but it is you, yourself, who is pushing you down. So, I believe there's still good in you," Empyrea spoke through Leo's voice while he shared the memories, shaking the dormant part of him in which he repressed.

He opened his eyes and stared blankly at Leo after realising his wrongdoing after opening his stone-cold heart to new perspectives. "I'm a monster. But my mistakes, my actions, has already incurred the destruction of several dimensions I've been to. It's too late to atone for my sins."

"It's not too late. Remember, with both our powers, we can travel through space and time to fix everything. However, we'll leave the path of destiny as it is, those which have already been routed for us, even if it means having to relive our shared, devastated past. Some things just can't be changed." With a helping hand, Leo lifted Lezaros to his feet.

After getting up Lezaros began guiding Leo on how he could locate someone in another dimension just by the thoughts of them, traversing and skipping dimensions without the need of passing through the dimensional Cusps. By using the powers of interdimensional travel in his grasp, he thought of his two missing friends and instantly appeared in front of Kyudo and Seiche as he travelled to and fro from their various 'lost', far away dimensions.

With both of them transported back to the Sylvian world to rejoin the rest of the Empyreans, Lezaros approached Leo and asked about locating Hades in the Multiverse next, but he insisted that they needed to fix everything else as their priority before they proceeded. They returned to the Sylvian Kingdom and used their powers to unfreeze time, and everything around them started to move as usual again.

As time resumed, both of Kyudo and Seiche turned around and leapt backwards, arming themselves to strike once they saw Lezaros behind him. Upon seeing him so close to Leo, the rest did the same. Without any delay, Ignis stepped in and froze him from the neck down, immobilising him from moving another inch.

"Hey! Stop!" Leo stood in front of Lezaros with his arms outstretched to the sides to defend him. "He's changed! Please unfreeze him."

After thawing him from his icy predicament, Leo revealed that Lezaros was actually his alternate dimensional counterpart. They walked forward together, regrouping with the rest and shared about what happened while they were gone. From far, upon noticing that everything was alright as if nothing had happened, Wendale emerged from his hiding spot to see what the commotion was about, still slightly afraid by the sight of Lezaros' face. Leo explained everything necessary, they understood more about Lezaros and the situation at the moment, but the whole ordeal was not over yet.

Leo and Lezaros looked at each other and nodded, understanding the mission through their visual cues on what they had to do next. With their powers, they began their dimensional restoration by first changing the past of the Sylvians, bringing back all of the ones who perished including King Nero who failed to vanquish Lezaros before during the first invasion of the kingdom. Ignis and her family were finally whole and reunited, expressing their gratitude before both of them continued onward.

Next, they began travelling through all the dimensions, fixing every single one of them until they reached the world of Horizon where they stopped momentarily, sighting Empyrea floating mid-air in front of where they appeared from the dimensional rifts.

"Leave it be. There's more to unfold in this world than meets the eye. Your mistake is merely a catalyst for this new reborn world," Empyrea's voice echoed through their heads while they thought. Both were speechless about her decisions, but they did as she said and left it in its new condition.

As they left Horizon, Lezaros informed Leo that they had two dimensions left to fix, the ones he had made significant changes in the past.

Reaching Neoteric City, they travelled back in time immediately upon arrival, a minute before Lezaros shook the very foundations of the city. They observed the skies where his past self had emerged from and waited with a plan in mind, their arms charged full of Empyrean magic. Seeing the dark clouds roll in, they knew it was a sign that he was arriving.

Just as *Past Lezaros* landed onto the ground from among the clouds, Leo whipped up a rift at his side while Lezaros blasted him through with all the magical charge he could muster, transporting him directly to the Alternate Felineatius dimension. With no time to spare, they hastily travelled there, only to see Past Lezaros rampaging around the towns. Joining their efforts together, they outpowered him and took care of him quickly by blasting him from two sides with strong waves of magic.

Ensuring that he could not retaliate and had been knocked out fully by poking around at his body, they conjured up a Spacetime seal, similar to the one Hades used to prevent Leo from saving him in the Incident. With the seal activated by their combined powers, he was permanently imprisoned in a bubble of magic. Upon awakening, he struggled to break out but was unable to dispel the duo's magic.

Once *Past Lezaros* was taken care of, they returned back to Neoteric City and reconstructed the past with their Empyrean magic and changed the future to what it was supposed to be. As they travelled back to the present, everything seemed the usual, full of flying cars and spaceships zooming around, bustling as it may be. Signs of life could be seen almost everywhere, indicating that they had fixed the past.

They strolled around the streets to observe if there were any anomalies as a result of their temporal modification of the past and began to notice residents running away from Lezaros screaming as they ran, while some frantically punched numbers into their holographic watches to inform the authorities.

"I guess we can't change their alternate memories of me striking them down on the streets..." he sighed as he thought of his bloodshed of the past.

Seeing that this was the only minor anomaly, both of them decided to leave it as it is.

"Leo, we need to head back to my dimension but deeper down the timeline to the moment before I corrupted myself with excess amounts of Empyrean powers. I'm not sure what we can do with my past self but let's try to correct him."

They travelled deeper into the past of Alternate Felineatius to the time before he drained Empyrean Shard of its energies and gained its powers. Once they set foot into the house, they burst into his bedroom and sighted *Past Lezaros* holding up the shard. Before *Past Lezaros* could siphon all its power, Leo knocked the Shard out of his hands and sent it deep into the sea of the Multiverse with a quick open and close of a rift in a blink of an eye, stopping him from corrupting his body with its concentrated Empyrean energies.

Lezaros gripped *Past Lezaros* by his shoulders tightly and shook him out of his trance, advising him not to be too greedy and just use the powers that he had already. Sharing his wisdom from his experiences, Leo stepped in and taught him the good in the world and guided him in his abilities. After a few days of observing *Past Lezaros* smoothly living his life while heeding his advice, both Leo and Lezaros decided that the future of Alternate Felineatius has changed.

Upon returning back to the present, they were surprised that it was still in one piece. Leo knew that Lezaros, as a fully realised Empyrean could protect Felineatius could defend the past from the destruction of the planet without the use of the Shard. But, little did Leo know that while they changed the past, the Lezaros from the other timeline would gradually fade out of existence due to a temporal paradox. Leo turned to look at him, horrified by the shape of his body slowly distorting intermittently into a translucent state, gradually dematerialising from the present.

"Leo, it was nice to be with you. I can't exist if the other me of the changed reality exists. I'm glad everything turned out more desirable than we ever could expect. Goodbye Leo..."

He witnessed Lezaros disappear in front of him and it left an impact on his heart, leaving his head hanging low. Before he could open a rift back to the Sylvian world, he felt a gentle tap on his shoulders. It was Lezaros, all grown up from the corrected past, but with the memories of the one whom he had just lost.

"I might not be the same Lezaros you knew before but I shall fulfil his one last, unfinished request - to find your companion,

Hades," he put his arm around him with a vague memory of being with Leo. One he opened a rift to the rest of the Empyreans, Lezaros followed him through the rift and both of them headed back together.

Once they returned to the Sylvian Kingdom, Leo tried to find Hades using his newfound dimensional travelling powers, he could not seem to open a rift to where he was in the Multiverse. Next, Lezaros attempted to assist him by opening the rift with him but their efforts returned fruitlessly, still unable to open the rift to his location.

"We're not able to reach him and I don't really know where he is. But, wherever he is isn't in reach, even with our combined powers. Your friend- I'm sorry, Leo..."

Leo collapsed onto the verdant, bentgrass hill behind him and buried his head in his hands. The fact that his momentary tinge of hope was immediately lost hit him in his gut like a sledgehammer. Seeing him saddened, Lezaros decided it was best to return back to Alternate Felineatius and leave him to accept the fate that was dawned on him.

That was it. He was not going to see Hades again even after he tried so hard. A dark cloud hung above his head as his despondent thoughts brought his mood down, making him progressively sadder.

Suddenly, another rift appeared in front of him, one which appeared different from the ones he could create from his powers. He lifted his head up to see what it was and saw three blue humanoid beings in white coloured cloaks appearing from the rift, one of them with golden-rimmed goggles strapped around its forehead.

"We are the fourth-dimensional Guardians of the Multiverse, seeker of truth and keeper of secrets. Come with us and we'll take you to whom you lost," the one with the goggles spoke with a deep and slightly raspy voice, beckoning the Empyreans and Wendale to follow.

They followed them through the rift into a place unknown, trusting in them that they could bring them to Hades eventually. Kadyn was slightly ambivalent and suspicious of them, having thoughts that it might be a trap and had her hands tightly gripped around her scimitars in preparation.

Chapter 10

(The Reunion)

Unlike the Cusping bridges that the Cuspers created before, the rift they passed through was a solid, whitish, light tunnel through a void, no falling or warping was taking place, only walking. Close to the end of the tunnel, Leo could make out an outline - a truncated-icosahedron shaped structure of sorts which had opalescent walls. As they entered, they could see many other Guardians and hexagonal holographic screens showing all the different dimensions with their inhabitants living their day-to-day lives in each of them.

"This is the centre of the Multiverse where beings like ourselves watch over all the plexus of dimensions in the thirty-two realms of the Multiverse. You see, we know of about the goings-on of mortals from dimension to dimension. To our eyes, your very existence a microcosm of the Multiverse," he stopped for a to wipe his golden-rimmed goggles before strapping it back on his forehead.

He explained that he would help Leo and the rest as a favour, mainly because he and his doppelganger restored most of the dimensions to their near-original state, lessening their eternal workload to fix the Multiverse. "And although we had some singularity rectifications here and there from the countless spacetime rifts you and your counterpart opened, along with other complicated spatial kinks and whatnots, that's not a big problem for us to set right. Give me a moment while I try to find your lost friend."

He raised his right hand and pressed it against a hexagonal holographic pane for a moment before lifting it off the holographic screen, shaking his head in uncertainty. "Where your friend is isn't in this specific plane of existence, but somewhere else beyond the reach of mortal interdimensional travel, or delving as you call it. So, there's a bit of a problem. I need a sample of his DNA to pinpoint his location or it might take more than your mortal lives for us to locate him in one of the countless dimensions."

"Uh-um... I-I do have some of his fur," Ignis stepped up confessed hesitantly. "I kept them in case we need it in some sort of seance to talk to Hades."

"That's kinda strange. Somethin' tells me ya like that li'l purply dude," Seiche poked at her.

"Yeah. It seems so obvious that you have feelings for him," Kadyn added, continuing to tease her.

"No, I'm not..." she blushed conspicuously while she vigorously shook her head and declined the fact. "I just wanted something to remember him by, okay!?"

She was trembling in embarrassment as she passed the sample to the Guardian, still a little anxious coming out of her comfort zone to disclose her secret stash, a sacrifice that she thought was worthwhile.

Using the DNA sample, the Guardian located where Hades was in a matter of seconds. "Hades is in dimension 3125, with reference to your Xenian Dimensional Database, on some place called 'Earth' past the border that distinguishes the true reality from fantasy, where all of you exist. Traveling through there would require tremendous amounts of energy to puncture a hole through the realms. Without that, the gap between would recoil dimensional forces on you, causing you to vanish from existence even before you get there."

Having said the problems to reach Hades, he suggested that they could temporarily use their Multiverse Warper to instantaneously travel to and fro, without the risk of getting their existence erased midway by the forces of the Multiverse during the journey there. He led them to a giant, gateway shaped apparatus that appeared like it was a technological grandeur in a way with its intricate designs, varying colours of lights that flash intermittently and wires twisted with the arch of the Warper. With the dexterous typing of several codes into the system, he fired up a portal, its edges gleaming from the radiant light of the opened rift and gusts of wind blowing from the other side.

'Hmm, I've not seen him in a long time and I wonder whether he would remember me...' He thought as he stared at the pulsating portal hesitantly. 'I can do this.'

Leo then took a deep breath and prepared himself to see Hades face to face again, hoping not to expect the worst. With his friends following closely behind his back, he was ready. They delved through the rift onto a grassy field where they could see Hades raising the Shard into the air in his paws while standing beside Empyrea and somebody else, glimmering brightly as he held it.

"Foxy?" Leo was tentative on whether that was really him and stood rooted in disbelief, thunderstruck on the sight of seeing him again after so long.

"Leo!" Hades leapt onto his body and hugged him, giving him the heartfelt ecstasy of long-lost reunion. Leo teared up while hugging him back, "it's been a long time, Foxy. A long time..."

"Too long..." He leaned his head against Hades', closing his eyes and relieved that he was doing fine.

The other Empyreans joined the duo and coalesced to hug him which made him squirm about in the midst of the group hug. After a while, they released him from the hug, he hopped back onto the ground, primping his fur back into its original, kempt condition. Wendale stood by the side smiling, glad that everything turned out as it should be.

"So... How exactly did you end up here, anyway? And most importantly, how did you actually retrieve the Shard from the explosion?" Leo asked in curiosity. "I thought you've perished in there."

"Well, it's a long story, a story for another time. I'll tell you all about it when we get back to Xenia. But before we go, I wanna bid my friend goodbye."

With a few final words and a hug to his friend, it was time to return.

And so, as their wearying search comes to a close, so too, does the story of the quest of reunion.

Part 1 Short Stories

Wendale, the First
Dimensional Delver

Wendale had a lifelong dream, a dream that one day he could visit other worlds - the other dimensions in the Multiverse, that is. Having been to countless planets in his early life, he felt that travelling to each one was turning mundane every trip as the places he went were already discovered a long time ago.

He wanted to do something more exciting, thinking of the existence of parallel universes and other dimensions, to feel like one of the first explorers that set foot on the planets he had been to if he were to explore these new planes of reality and unlocked its secrets.

Upon entering the Xenian Intergalactic Federation, he was admitted into the research group which studied the properties of the dimensions that forms the primary foundations of the Multiverse. He was slightly disappointed after realizing that he was not going to be the first to discover the new worlds, learning that interdimensional travel has been invented.

The only way they could travel across the Cusp was to use the bulky Cusp-Delver machine brought over to them from Neoteric City. He and some of the other researchers were only able to cross the Cusp of Xenia up to two neighbouring dimensions using the machine. However, it was not even convenient to operate them, requiring massive amounts of energy and portals on either end to stabilize the Cusping Bridges, spatial tunnels which link the Cusps together. This small inconvenience gave him an idea to change this way of travel, an open door of opportunity for him to step into and innovate.

His plan of action was to develop a device that was capable of travelling Cusps easily, with a goal in mind to revolutionize the means of interdimensional travel. He racked his brain and researched for months, but he could not think of any other way to cross the Cusps remotely without the use of these machines. Even with Paulson's help to hypothesize such an unorthodox gadget, they still could not figure it out.

In between worlds, he would pass through the Cusping Bridges, but never once did he probe around in the tunnels. Without much data of the Cusps to go by, he decided to start from scratch to pursue an expedition to explore these tunnels and prepared for months on end for the next step in his research.

With a compact turbo-jetpack, he entered the tunnel, drifting in the whitish void with a holographic scanner in his right paw. He instructed the other scientists to close the rift after he entered, knowing that he was risking his life as he might not return, to further his discoveries for Xenia's glory without a second thought - as a literal lab rat.

While he moved the scanner around, he was picking up different levels of energy, fluctuating as he shifted it about. As he inched the scanner towards the areas where there were significantly higher levels of energy, he discovered an iridescent crystalline structure stuck into the walls of the white void tunnel, scattered all about in isolated corners.

Wendale could not believe his eyes, a new discovery and a new specimen of an unknown element. He reached his paws towards one, yanked it out of the tunnel wall and examined it scrupulously with the aid of his scanner. However, the scanner could not identify what kind of compositions it had, showing a "null" on the holographic display, confirming his guesses that it was comprised of an undiscovered element.

'This mysterious element must have something to do with travelling the Cusp. I must find a way to get back to report this to the Federation,' he thought. Still floating in the white void, he searched his pockets for his tools and started fiddling with the crystal sample. But to no avail, he could not figure out a way to utilize the crystal.

Thinking that he would be stuck in the void for an eternity, he took out his spectacle cloth to clean off the smudge on the sample that he had while he waited for something to happen. As he tried to clean the sample, a static spark discharged from the cloth, causing a rift to appear in the void. The rift revealed a familiar scene - the corner of the lab where the Cusp and Multiverse researchers were.

'Huh,' he thought. With another shock, the rift sealed up and disappeared completely.

'Ah. I think I've got it.' He shocked it once again and the rift re-opened. In one huge burst of propulsion from his jetpack, jolting himself back into the laboratory and crashed into a few stools as he re-entered the Xenia. He stood up and brushed the dust of his body, still trying to catch his breath from the excitement of discovery that he had.

"Dale, how did you get back without the help of Cusp-Delver? I was gonna save you in a few hours if you didn't return! How is this possible?" Paulson asked with both his eyes wide open from the shock he got when Wendale crashed beside him.

"It was simple, Paws."

He explained long-windedly about his findings and discovery could allow Xenians to travel through Cusps quicker. When Paulson requested Wendale to recreate what he just did, he took an igniter from a close-by table and positioned it close to the crystal in his paw. He began to demonstrate the properties of the crystal, showing how the rifts open and close through a series of shocks. Paulson suggested that he needed name this unknown element, making it official as a big discovery.

"Cuspmium. I think it is apt to give it that name considering that I found it in the Cusp and it has a nice ring to it," Wendale proclaimed, his paw pointed up into the air as he thought of its name.

After a few months worth of experimental records were done on Cuspmium, Paulson recommended that they needed to travel back to the origin of interdimensional travel - Neoteric City, where the Cusp-Delver was invented, to develop something out of Cuspmium since Xenia did not have that scale of technology to do so. If they were to share their discoveries and numeral concepts with the Neoterians, their method of interdimensional travel would be improved. With a mutual agreement between the two on the idea, Paulson calibrated the portal destination on the Cusp-Delver to Neoteric City.

"And set! Dale, the rift is fired up to bring us to Neoteric City. Let's go shall we?" Paulson invited with the gesture of his paw, beckoning Wendale to follow along quickly.

As they stepped through the portal into Neoteric City, they took a walk towards the central building of the city where all technological marvels are created, the Technological Hub. With the help of other Neoterians, they began to utilise the Cuspmium crystals and went through a long slew of experimentation, recreating their theories on the element through testing the properties and capabilities of each crystal.

Finally, they made a wristband-like gadget which allowed them to travel dimensions at the positions where the Cusps were in a snap, ensued from a whole Neoteric year of hard work. They coined it, the "Transdimensional Cusper", or "Cusper" in short, the first remote Multiverse travel device without the need of transporting a hefty load of migrating an interdimensional machine every time they travelled to somewhere new. When the first few Cuspers were produced, Wendale led the team along with Paulson into the other dimensions, calling themselves, the Dimensional Delvers, who delves deep into the Multiverse into other worlds alike or unique to their world.

As they passed through each one, they recorded their features into the database, but with the limitation of charges of the Cuspmium crystal, they had to return after multiple dimensions before the crystals shattered. While they stopped after a few, the Neoterians continued forward to the extreme ends and numbered everything, allocating the dimensional numbers 0 to 3000. Xenia was numbered as Dimension 622 in the Xenian Dimensional Database, one of the transit waypoints dimensions to restock on supplies for the Delvers.

Because none of the Neoterians could pass the dimensional Cusps of Dimension 0 or 3000 even with the abundance of Cuspmium crystals they had been provided, they named the phenomenon, the "Delver's Edge of the Dimensions", a dead-end in their record for the Multiverse Database. Unfortunately, going to such extent of research meant sacrifices. Many who reached these edges could not return or perished on the journey back, lost forever in the dimensions, but their priceless data recorded in the Multiverse Database was well worth the sacrifice for the future of interdimensional travel.

A couple of years later, with the technology introduced to Xenia, word of his discovery disseminated throughout the galaxies. He was known for being the trailblazer of interdimensional travel in rapid succession, his dimensional delving team, and most of all, the thing that started it all, the discovery of Cuspmium.

Years had gone by as they travelled annually into the other realms to record the changes, eventually leading the Neoterians to create an entire Multiverse map system to simplify the routes by using shortcuts while travelling to the dimensions themselves.

Wendale and the Rebirth of Horizon

Upon crossing the Cusping Bridge from Neoteric City, he set foot onto a path cutting past a small hill encircled by the verdures which seemed like a refreshing hue of green paint splattered onto a rocky canvas. While he was there to do some further research and detailed observation, he was also there to additionally explore the world and record anything interesting that he could find in the new world.

Around where he started, he set up a data transponder onto the ground and activated it with a few presses of the hexagonal holographic panel. It was left hidden in the midst of a dense thicket, shrouded by the small leaves and branches so that no other living creatures of the unexplored world could disrupt its functions while it scanned. Placing it down, it sent energy pulses around its proximity and picked up a few life signatures, one being the closest around the hill.

He trekked his way through the hills and came across a thatch-roofed cottage with constant billows of smoke rising slowly into the air. Curious about the inhabitant inside, he peered through the windows but he could not see anyone. He knocked on the door gently, hoping that someone was in. Almost immediately, it burst open with so much force that he could feel a strong gust of wind hit his face, taken aback by it. Before he could react, a pair of beefy hands dragged him through and he felt his body get crushed whilst being hugged by a heavily built figure.

"Hello, new face. Welcome to me blacksmith cottage, yer li'l fluffy lad. Do yer want anythin'? Snacks or whiskey? Ye can call me Brander, the Bovinean, the best of smiths yer ever be gettin' in yer face."

After he was released, he took a moment to catch his breath and straighten up his lab coat, preparing himself for a proper introduction. "Hello there, I'm Wendale, a scientist from Xenia, or you could call me Dale in short. Thank you for the warm welcome. I'm just wandering the world and thought that I'd stop by to learn more about this place and what goes around here. Maybe you could give me some insight into the goings-on in this place?"

"Ya mean Horizon? Aye, I can tell ye all about Horizon if ya want, yer li'l outsider. Sit right next to me and I'll tell ya all about it!" Brander said excitedly as he shoved Wendale into a chair and started to share the tales about how it was named after the beautiful dawns and dusks, and all the great things about Horizon until it turned dark outside. As it was too dark to observe anything, he requested an accommodation in the cottage a night or two. Without any hesitation, Brander offered him a whole week of staying over and said that he was welcomed to visit anytime, as he was being a pleasant guest there.

While he was at his cottage, he heard all sorts of stories from Horizon's legends and some ghost stories about a wandering black shadow - the Shadow of Horizon, one of the legends that got Wendale intrigued. Every time Brander talked about the Shadow, he asked more about it, but little was known of this mysterious entity, he who comes and goes in the night.

"The Shadow, it's still around till this day, wanderin' and freakin' the heck out of the people I told the scary spooks to, includin' you. Well, we'll never know what he's gonna do, yer know."

"He doesn't seem too scary to me. I mean, I haven't seen him yet," Wendale replied.

"Don't worry, li'l lad, you'll see him one of these nights."

After a week of research and staying over at the cottage, he decided to return back to Xenia to record all of his research. "Haste yer back, li'l 'un. It's a pleasure talkin' to ya. Hope ye got everythin' yer needed!" Brander yelled as Wendale departed the cottage, bidding goodbye to him for the moment.

On the next visit to Horizon, he went around the hills surrounding Brander's cottage to scan the surroundings for any distinct changes with the climate and environment. While wandering around, he appreciated the reddish-orange splatter on the dark blue backdrop, distracted and oblivious to the giant rock beneath his feet. As he kicked the inconspicuous rock, he tripped and tumbled down the hill, stopping abruptly after colliding with a tree.

He laid flat, face-up on the ground and thought, 'ah... Since I'm already lying down, I might as well sleep here tonight. It's nice to camp out once in a while. This is my life now, heh heh,' he chuckled to himself under his breath, turning the slight misfortune he had into a bit of laughter. The night began to fall and he became sleepy, his eyelids were gradually shutting. But something was sending chills down through his tailbone and the fur on his back stood straight up. He could sense that something was not right.

It turned slightly brighter for a moment and darkened again before another glaring flash of light shone in the distance. Wendale immediately got up to his feet and saw a blackish outline hovering around a glowing orb of red pulsating energy. He gasped and identified it as the Shadow of Horizon that Brander was talking about and watched speechless as he began to make the orb grow bigger until it exploded, sending reddish shockwaves of intense energy in his direction.

Instinctively, he saw it as a cataclysmic event unfolding before him and began to frantically tap on the "activate" button on his Cusper to escape the world into Neoteric City. Opening a rift, he slipped through and closed the rift swiftly. He sighed in relief, a close call from death managing to evacuate Horizon in time.

When he re-entered Horizon, it was broken up into small floating chunks, remnants of the world that it once was which floated without a known reason. He was transfixed momentarily by the stark alteration of the world, but he sought to find a theoretical reason why.

He hypothesized that something else has been altered other than the physical changes as far as his eye could see. Being curious about what it could be, he did a scan with his gadgets again and discovered that something had indeed changed. There were psionic energies flowing everywhere throughout the air, causing the islands to float instead of imploding into oblivion after the explosion.

He went towards his data transponder in the bushes and was shocked that it stayed intact through the whole event. However, it indicated that a third of the number of life signatures were still active. "Hmm... About one third survived the catastrophe," he mumbled while keying it down in his holographic notepad. With his database on Horizon updated, he felt like he had forgotten something. He thought hard for a moment before something hit him on the head like a hammer on an anvil.

'Brander!' He thought, worried that he was caught in the cataclysm and something might have happened to him in the span of time he was absent. As quickly and as carefully as he could, he leapt from island to island to get to Brander's cottage and saw that it was still in one piece. He was utterly amazed and puzzled that whatever that blew up did not destroy everything but he wanted to double-check anyway.

He entered the cottage only to see Brander napping peacefully with a hammer in hand and a pair of crucible tongs clasping on a cooled piece of metal in the other, appearing like he was midway through hammering something before he fell asleep. He heaved a sigh of relief to see him still well and alright. Wendale went forward to shake him up from his slumber, questioning him whether he saw the explosion happen. He declined about having to know of any kind of explosion.

When he stepped out of his cottage, his heart skipped a beat, his mouth agape in astonishment with his right hand on the horns of his head. Seeing the world around him change with a purplish dawn backdrop was like awakening from the clanging sounds of his own hammer. While he was still trying to fathom out what actually took place, Wendale decided it would be best to leave him to process the changes slowly at his own time.

"Um, I think I'll leave you be. I guess I'll visit you again soon Brander."

"Uh-huh..." he muttered under his breath, scratching the back of his head as he was still aghast at what had happened and was rooted in position at the doors of the cottage.

Faye the Orphan

Born to Vulpine parents on the world of Horizon, Faye was named after her white fur, a colour that stood out from the normal hue of orange, unlike most of her species, appearing as if she was touched by the magic of fairies. From birth, she did not enjoy staying in the company of others, especially strangers from other races whom she did not recognise. She would hide behind her parents whenever someone enters the house, naturally defensive about her personal space, bashful and introverted.

As she grew, she loved to caper around her home, wide and extensive farmland cultivating fruits and berries, where a forest of bearing fruit trees and berry shrubs encircled her house. Butterflies and other creatures would occasionally visit and Faye would usually prod them curiously with her paws, or chase the birds that would perch on the fence surrounding her home, giving her the joys of her childhood. However, while she felt that she was at the peak of happiness, little did she know it was going to be short-lived.

One evening, as Faye skipped around the flowering shrubs, she heard a deafening explosion from behind her ears. She turned around, only to see her mother rushing towards her, grabbing her by the paws and pulled her in the opposite direction of their home. Faye wanted to question why she was taken away from home but could not ask at that moment as she was trying to catch her breath from running.

With the shockwave of the explosion still yet to come, Faye's mother thought it would be safer if they hid in a cave and waited out, bringing her towards a mountain cave close to the blacksmith's cottage. Upon entering the cave, Faye's mother collapsed onto the ground and started weeping. "Faye, h-he didn't make it."

Faye took a moment before she the same sense of devastation hit her, realising that her father was gone forever. While in her mother's embrace, both of them lost track of time and dozed off while the intense wave of the explosion swept by the entrance, levelling small trees and shrubs in the open.

When they awoke the next morning, they were taken aback to see what once was a rocky hill turning into broken islands which floated above a void of nothingness. Following her mother towards the blacksmith's cottage, they leapt past the gaps between the floating islands towards a straw-capped cottage with a trail of dense, rising smoke streaming from its chimney. Unfortunately, as they got closer, the island they were on began to tremor violently, suddenly sinking into the void.

"Head for the cottage and whatever you do, don't look back!" She shouted with all her breath as she heaved Faye up onto another island before the island she was on plummeted into the void below. As she stood back up and turned back, she was horrified to learn that her mother, too, was gone in an instant. Following her mother's last instruction, she ran towards the cottage for cover. She was surprised that the cottage managed to withstand the shockwave, even though it did not appear sturdy.

However, when she arrived at the cottage, she could not handle the physical and emotional fatigue that overwhelmed her and blacked out before her paws could ever reach the doorknob. After regaining consciousness, she discovered that she was on somebody's bed, definitely not her own. She glanced around the room that she was in and sighted someone with horns, polishing a metallic blade. "Aye, ye li'l foxy 'un, yer finally awake. Name's Brander, the Bovinean Blacksmith."

Startled by the burly frame of Brander and the shiny metal blade he was carrying, she wrapped her tail around her face and huddled below the blankets, withdrawn from her constant fear of new strangers.

"No need to be afraid young 'un. I'm a childhood friend of yer mother's and I won't hurt ye. Make yerself at home. Just take whatever yer need to make yerself comfortable."

Gradually, she got used to seeing Brander stomp around on his hooves carrying heavy metallic items while she explored the cottage of his, slowly beginning to open up to him as she felt her anxiety dissipate by the minute.

A few days later, she felt comfortable about sharing the pain she had to endure with Brander, allowing him to understand the circumstances she was in. He understood her pain and decided it would be best if he took care of her rather than letting her run aimlessly around the floating islands without proper care, allowing her to live with him from then on. She began to settle down into her new home, adjusting to the significant changes to her life.

In the evening two weeks after the fateful day, she wandered around the area outside Brander's cottage, throwing rocks into the void to see if anything happened. As she threw rocks down into the void, she saw that one of the rocks she threw had whitish glowing outlines, floating midair and not falling into the void. She waved her paw to the sides and the rock followed her paw, shaking it from side to side, gradually waving faster until it was propelled off the edge of the floating island.

She gasped in amazement. Did she do that? Faye knew that she had a gift, a newfound power developed from the aftermath of the explosion - a gift of hope and change. Soon, she tried all sorts of tricks from day to day, flinging rocks into the sky before shattering them with her powers into small fragments and dust that rained like fireworks all around her.

As the weeks passed, her powers grew exponentially stronger. To test the capabilities of her recently developed power, she would often try them out on Brander, causing him to feel slightly disturbed but not irritated over being a test subject for Faye. She would hypnotise him from time to time and speak through his head with reverberating telepathic voices, freaking him out while he was napping. Her psionic abilities allowed her to surpass the limitations of living normally.

Finally, as she grasped the mastery of her psionic powers, she could fly around without restriction, feeling the freedom that she always wanted. She was ready to take on any challenges that awaited her in the near future. But there were still unanswered questions on her mind as she thought about the past. 'What was down in the void? And, were her parents still down there?'

She peered into the void for a moment. Eventually, curiosity took the better of Faye as she dove straight down into the void. The deeper she went, the darker it became and soon it was a complete pitch-black. She wondered if she could still find her parents if she dove deeper, but she realised she was not alone.

There was something in the dark. A scintillating dot from afar was pulsating and began to grow in size and brightness. As it got closer, she was stunned and with no way to dodge it, she was hit by an intense sphere of energy, encapsulating her in the sphere where her powers were nullified. She was in a bubble of light, floating through the dark abyss.

"What's this?" She spoke to herself, wondering about what she had been trapped into.

"Faye, you are the first and soon-to-be strongest psychic to utilize the psionic forces flowing throughout the rebirthed world of Horizon. You mustn't get swamped by the darkness of the void by going deeper for the ones you sought. They're lost forever, but, with every loss comes opportunities to change. Grow your powers and reshape the future of Horizon into a more desirable and hospitable one. Lead others in the world with similar abilities to you and together, there shall be peace and harmony. For now, I will return you back to where you came from." A sombre, female voice resounded all throughout the bubble of light.

Immediately after the voice stopped, the sphere popped and turned into a blinding light, and in a split second, she was teleported back into the cottage, in her bed where Brander was sitting beside her. She rubbed her eyes and yawned, trying to figure out how she ended up in the bed if she did leave the cottage. Maybe it was a dream?

"Hey li'l 'un, I don't know how yer appeared at the doorstep out of nowhere, but ye should probably rest. Go back to sleep and I'll be with you later," he said as he caressed her forehead and ears gently before leaving her room.

Just as she laid down, she heard a knock on the door. As curiosity kicked in, she viewed through the gaps her room door and saw Brander open the door to a group of strangers, varying in sizes and appearances. She sneaked into the living room and hid behind Brander's workbench, curious to see the unfamiliar faces. At the same time, she was shy and began to hug her tail close to her cheeks.

"Dale?" Brander uttered in disbelief, seeing his old friend visit him again with new faces.

PART 2

Hades' Earthly Escapade

(The Incident)

After knocking Asmodia out, a menacing Asmodian demon queen, the Empyreans discussed how they were going to deal with the rest of the Asmodian armada who could wipe out the universe with the Empyrean energy extracted from the Shard. Hades thought it would be better if he transformed into Paulson, who was a genius and a brilliant inventor of the Intergalactic Federation. And thinking like a genius through his shapeshifting powers could help them in their cause to solve the insurmountable problem of dealing with a planet-filled with Asmodians ready to wreak havoc around the galaxy on her signal.

While transformed into the genius himself and additionally gaining intelligence into his mind, Hades turning pensive to come out with an idea, like how Paulson would usually think. As he thought deeper, there were only two feasible ways to take care of the remaining Asmodian armada - the first way is to try to purge all the massive Empyrean energy charges from the ships and prevent Xenia's invasion, in which there was insufficient time to execute. It would be seemingly impossible to remove all the Empyrean energy from every weapon and ship before they knew what was going on and began their attack.

The second idea, a reckless idea, was to eliminate the entire Asmodian armada before they even left by annihilating their home planet as a whole by overloading the power condenser of the Empyrean energy extractor. This would cause a chain reaction, detonating anything containing the Empyrean energies like explosive charges, capable of clearing out the armada effectively.

Asmodia, who had been silently eavesdropping on their conversation behind their backs while she laid on the floor, slowly got up and leaned onto the control systems of the Empyrean energy extractor, gripping onto a red lever lined with yellow and black tape.

"If I die, you'll all die with me!" She scowled, pulling the lever on the controls, setting the contraption to overload. With his swift reaction, Leo launched another wave of magic, quelling her for good after her supposed death. He attempted to shift the lever back but ended up breaking it, leaving it in its stuck position.

Observing that the powers of the Shard were growing erratically, Hades knew that it going to explode any time soon. He then decided, since the contraption was placed on overload anyway, nothing was going to change his determination to execute the second plan. He transformed into Leo and made use of an imitation of his intense mystic powers to attempt to contain the burst of energy from the detonation, encapsulating it in a strong magical sphere.

Although he could restrain its explosive energy, it was only a temporary solution, leaving Hades in a quandary. He was stuck between a rock and a hard place. If he released its energies to run, they would all perish in an instant, including the rest of the Empyreans, his treasured friends. However, if he stayed, his sacrifice could buy time for the rest of the Empyreans to escape, but this meant he would perish in the process.

While containing the fluctuating and unstable energies, he decided to stay behind, requesting Leo and the Empyreans to find a spaceship and get off the planet while he restrained the force of the explosion.

"But..." Leo immediately protested at his choice. "Foxy, no you can't-"

"Please confide in what I'm doing. Goodbye, fellow Empyreans," With a teardrop flowing down his cheek, he used his power to whisk all of them onto a nearby demon ship and teleported them deep into space, far away from the reaches of the oncoming explosion.

Alone accompanied by the low humming sound of the pulsating energy he held, he watched the glowing encapsulation of energy in front of him, gradually becoming a struggle to contain it. While transformed into Leo, he was able to share Leo's current thoughts and realized that he might return back in time to sacrifice himself instead by doing exactly what he did, changing the whole timeline completely.

With that possible scenario thought in his mind, Hades, in Leo's image, whipped up a powerful time spell with one paw while still holding onto the immense energy of the contraption with the other. He conjured up a cosmic temporal seal, restricting anyone from time-travelling to that exact space and time.

Just as he initiated the spell, Empyrea's spectral projection appeared beside him and she placed her paw on his shoulder.

"Do as you must for this is all predestined to happen. Your sacrifice shall never be forgotten..." She spoke to him as she faded away, her voice reverberating around the room gradually turning silent, only the constant rumbling of the containment could be felt.

As the Empyreans were far enough away from the planet, and he felt ready, Hades closed his eyes, releasing the grasp on the immense energy he held and the contraption exploded with a blinding light. He stood with his arms outstretched, ready to embrace his end. However, during the explosion, some of its Empyrean energy wrapped around him like a cocoon, protecting him from the dangers of perishing. As the lights were becoming too bright, he failed to see that he was being transported somewhere else instead of dying to its energies.

The intensity of the light was so strong that neither his eyelids nor paws could shield his eyes, causing him to pass out immediately due to the overwhelming visual stimulation.

Chapter 1

(Reawakening Into the Unknown World)

As he awoke, he glanced around him to see where he had ended up. 'Where am I?' He wondered. 'Am I in heaven?' Still slightly puzzled, he tried pinching himself on the paw. He felt a certain bit of pain, which meant he was neither in a dream nor heaven. He was somewhere. But where? His mind was filled to the brim with thoughts and questions, distracting himself from the situation presently.

Oblivious that he was sitting on the canopies of a tall tree, the branch he was resting on suddenly snapped and he tumbled through leaves and branches, causing him to crash onto the foliage of the underbrush, which cushioned his fall.

"Oof!" He spurted out upon landing onto the leaf-covered ground amidst the lush shrubbery. While brushing off the leaves and dirt from the fur on his body, he checked his body and tail, discovering that he was completely unscathed, surprisingly not even a scratch. Next, he attempted to shapeshift, but nothing happened when he tried to transform into Leo. 'Hmm... That's strange,' he thought. 'My powers don't seem to work here.'

When he attempted to speak, only shrills emanated from his snout. He figured that in the world he was in, there were others like him, but they spoke a different language from what he was used to. He sighed and decided it was best to find out where he was first before learning the native language there through his shapeshifting powers.

Scanning the area around him, he was somewhere in a forest clearing with metallic debris from the energy siphoning contraption strewn across the ground. One thing stood out - something of a blue tint was glistening from within the dirt. It was of no doubt, the glow from Empyrean Shard. Hades thought that it had been destroyed in the explosion, but with a shrug, he decided not to think of the possibilities on how it stayed intact through the whole incident.

As he reached out for it with his paws, a yellow beam was shot just a few inches shy of his fur on his arm, quickly retracting it away in time. Instinctively, he took to the heels and scampering off as fast as he could, taking a glimpse of his assailant over his shoulder. Someone dressed in black was trying to gun him down, but he was swift enough to get away from the vicinity, ending up deep in a pine forest where he found a small trench to hide for the time being.

While crouched down in the trench, he made himself invisible to his assailant who ran across the trench right above his head without noticing him. Once his attacker had left his area, he climbed out of the trench and heaved a sigh of relief, laying his body against the white bark of a close-by pine tree, his head leaning back as his eyes closed in exhaustion.

"Hey, you there!" The feminine voice came in the form of a shrill, but somehow, Hades could make sense of it, popping his eyes wide open immediately. He turned to face the source of the voice and to his astonishment, there was a quadrupedal fox staring at him, the first fox he saw on fours which were unlike any of his friends he knee on his home planet. "Name's Amber! What's your's, weird-looking fox?"

"H-hi, I'm Hades. I'm lost and I need to find a way out of this forest so that I might get a sense of direction around this place, a vantage point if there is any. Could you lead me out of the forest?" He requested using a series of yaps.

"Aight! Just get on my back and I'll bring you to the forest edge. While we're at it, I wanna ask you some questions too! I'm kinda curious about you, interesting fella."

As Hades clambered onto her back, Amber found him to be surprisingly light and could carry his weight around easily to take him where he wanted to go. Smiling, she happily weaved through the pines and ledges, heading towards the forest's edge.

"So, why are you purple and how are you able to stand on two?"

"Where I was born, the creatures alike come in all shapes and colours, but all of us walk on twos naturally."

As they continued moving, she began to share about how foxes like her live their lives and such. Soon, she stopped in her footsteps for a while to take a small break from moving around, scouting the best possible path out of the forest. "By the way, you walk like a human, which is unlike any of the other friends I have in the forest. You're unique and weird, just the way I like it!"

Hades was curious about what a human was and asked her about them.

"Oh, they're basically just a bunch of arrogant, evolved monkeys who think that they dominate the world as the smartest creatures." Amber continued to babble about how they behaved in their community and enthused him in learning more about humans. Eventually, they reached the edge of the forest and they had to split.

"Here's the border between human-land and the whitebark pines where my kind lives. Just take caution to all humans. As foxes ourselves, we'll always tend to avoid them because we do not know their actual intentions. So, be careful, okay?"

"Yep! You got it!"

With the last piece of advice given, Hades set off through the borderline into the unknown world, wondering what is in store for him. The thought of who or what a human could be intrigued him. It seemed like his only choice was to begin interacting with them so as to get their help to return to where he came from.

While travelling downhill with his tail swaying about, he felt a presence behind him from the tingling sensation from the tip of his tail. From the corner of his eye, he could see the same assailant he had encountered before, still in hot pursuit of him, spotting the instant he was in Hades' vicinity.

As the gap between them gradually closed up, Hades had no choice but to go on all fours and make haste to prevent his assailant from catching up. However, while he tried his best to skitter away, he was oblivious about the assailant pulling out a tranquilizer gun, arming it behind him silently as he ran. With one shot of the tranquilizer energy beam landing a hit on his leg, he felt it beginning to give in to the beam's effect.

While still going strong, he ran with a limp and abruptly turned a corner, sliding himself to one side and hiding in a thick bush nearby. Beneath the verdure of the leaves, he was well concealed, seeing that his assailant run past where he was once more, continuing on a wild goose chase for him. Even though the chase for him was over, he could feel his lungs aching from it as he lay amidst the leaves to catch his breath.

After catching his breath, he inspected his legs, noticing a slight singe on his right leg where the tranquilizer beam hit, unable to bend or move slightly as it turned fully numb. In addition to the numbness, a throbbing headache developed as the full after-effects started to kick in, keeping him in a constant state of torment. He stared at the ground in front of him with his bleary eyes, trying to keep himself awake while going against the induced drowsiness of the beam.

As the skies turned dark, he staggered his way through the clearing onto an asphalt surface. While he followed the road, he could see a pair of lights in the distance, appearing as if someone was there and light was reflecting off their eyes. Rubbing his eyes to make sure he was not hallucinating, the lights were still there, gradually becoming too bright for his eyes.

Using his paws to shade his eyes, he walked towards the lights. He was slightly delirious from the after-effects of the beam and was unaware of it, hoping that the lights were someone or something who could provide help and give him refuge.

Unfortunately, as the pair of lights came too close, he discovered that it was a car and stared blankly like a deer in the headlights, unable to react quick enough to the oncoming vehicle. He was thrown forward by the force of the collision and was knocked out immediately as he fell onto the road a distance away.

Chapter 2

(Unsettling Truths)

The car screeched to a halt once Hades was knocked over, stopping by the roadside a few feet away from where he lay. With his drooping eyelids, he had one last glimpse of two shadowy figures approaching him slowly, one comparatively shorter than the other, coming to attend to him.

Upon being found, Hades' face appeared to be pallid, as if all the soul from his body has been drained. He could sense that he was lifted into the small arms of a girl, innocent with a pure heart, by some instinctive feeling. Knowing that he would be safe for a while, he closed his eyes and left his life in her hands.

"Quick, Casey! We'll need to bring this one to my sanctuary as soon as possible!"

"Alright, dad!"

She carried him and paced her way to the car as fast as she could. While being carried in her arms, Hades' arms dangled around as if it were made of jelly. His head, legs, and tail laid against the shoulders of the girl in a comfortable position, reducing the amount of suffering he was having at that moment in time. Leaving no time to delay, they hurriedly rushed Hades towards the Wildlife Protection Sanctuary, which was just a stone's throw away from their current location.

Reaching the sanctuary within minutes, they made their move towards the veterinary clinic. As Hades was nestled in the girl's arms, it brought him warmth and he regained some bit of consciousness, enabling to squint minimally to see what was happening. However, he was still unable to move any part of his body.

As he was rushed into the emergency nursing room, Casey's father quickly strapped on a pair of rubber gloves and examined him from head to tail. He lifted each leg to discover that there was a small patch of burnt up fur on his right leg. Upon further inspection, it did not seem serious to him at all.

"He looks fine to me. It's just a flesh wound from a burn, probably from wildfire or leftover campfires left smoldering and unextinguished. Let's see if he's hurt anywhere else..."

After shifting his limbs around and pinching certain muscles to check for any maiming injury, he found Hades to be completely alright, on the road to recovery. Standing beside him as a "handy assistant", Casey prodded his paw pads as her father flipped over the injured leg.

"Really? Must you always do that every time you meet my new patients?"

She giggled childishly. "Nope! I just wanted to test how squishy this purple mutated fox's paws are compared to the ones we helped in the past. C'mon, it's not like we would see a mutated fox every day!"

"It doesn't seem to be mutated. I'm afraid this might just be some purple-coloured dye," he stated truthfully with a dash of regret, pulling out a cotton swab and a bottle of surgical spirit solution to disinfect the wound.

After finishing the necessary treatments, he attempted to prove that his colouration was only purple dye by applying the alcoholic solution on a patch of fur on his back, rubbing against the fur in a gentle, circular motion to clean away the "dye" on his fur. Seeing that it did not work, he tried again with just a few strands. Despite his endeavours, the fur on his back did not even slightly discolour one bit, which only meant one thing - it was his real fur colour.

Being astounded, he saw Hades as a unique specimen of an undiscovered, "new" species of fox and was curious to learn more. But as of his condition at the moment, he decided that both he and Casey left the room to allow him to rest for a bit before their next course of action.

Throughout the conversation, Hades was squinting inconspicuously and secretly eavesdropping on them, trying to learn more about them while he was partially conscious.

'Hmm, that girl who carried me here, Casey, seems like someone kind that I could rely on to help me,' he thought, without second guessing himself. With his eyes half-open, he transformed into her for an instant before reverting to his foxy form, learning about her language and whereabouts in the world he was in through his shapeshifting powers. "Ah. Now, I can speak like a human. First of all, I'll need to find Casey."

As he stepped off the bed onto the cold, polished marble floors, he felt the burden of lethargy all over his body, but he could still manage to hold on to his consciousness for a while. Stealthily, he sneaked out of the nursing room and hobbled his way out of the veterinarian building, almost instantly sighting Casey in the distance past a few enclosures.

With every struggling step taken, the previously tumultuous animals in each enclosure that he passed by turned dead silent as soon as they saw him as if he was some sort of freak which they were afraid of. As this change happened noticeably, Casey shifted her gaze and stared vacantly as she sighted Hades limping on two, closing in on where she stood.

But as he approached her, he could feel his legs trembling unsteadily beneath him, barely able to support the weight of his own body anymore as the drowsiness came into play. At the very last moment, he stumbled on his foot and keeled over onto Casey's legs, grasping it for support for a split second before his vision went black.

Upon witnessing the scene unfold before his very eyes, her father remarked, "It seems he has taken a liking to you, Casey. But…"

"Can we keep him, pretty please? It's a once in a lifetime opportunity to care for a fox! Much less, it's a special one!"

He sighed and thought hesitantly for a moment. Having the purple fox at home was an opportunity to observe him more closely while taking care of him, killing two birds with one stone. "Maybe for a while, I guess. But once he's all better, we'll set him free, back to his natural habitat."

Casey held Hades in her arms in excitement, cradling him with her warmth while they sauntered back to the car for the last leg of the journey home. When she entered the car, Hades mumbled under his breath with his eyes still closed shut, "I feel so woozy," and then, he became silent once more.

"Dad, d-did he just speak?" Casey asked in astonishment, her eyes open in amazement.

"Animals can't talk, Casey. And it's late and you might just be frazzled after all the commotion we had in the sanctuary today. Maybe you're imagining it."

"Hmm..." She uttered in a slightly irritated tone. She was annoyed and began to tousle the tufts of fur on his head with her fingers as she pouted, believing that it was not her imagination. She swore that did hear it! But as an imaginative twelve-year-old, there was nothing to convince her father otherwise.

When Hades finally roused from his slumber, he rubbed his eyes with his paws and blinked, glancing about to see where he had ended up. He was in some kind of miniature bed lined with a comfy warm cotton padding and a mini velvet blanket. As he sat up, he felt that the fur on his head was somewhat dishevelled, which could only mean that he was out cold for a long time.

But how long? It did not matter to him as this was not the most important thing at the moment in time to worry about. With a few shakes from side-to-side, it returned to its neat and tidy position. Sniffing the air around him in curiosity, he could smell perfume, namely floral perfumes which were scents he could not recognise.

"Where am I?" He asked himself aloud, thinking that he was alone in the room.

"You're in my room. And whew! I knew I wasn't imagining that you could talk."

She startled him from behind as he tried to stand up, falling back onto his rear, his legs still slightly numb from waking.

"My name is Hades. I can talk, and it's no big deal," he introduced himself with a shrug as he stood back up on two. "Nice to meet you too, Casey."

"W-Wait! Hold on a second! First of all, how are you able to walk on two and talk? Foxes here aren't supposed to do any of those. Secondly, how did you know my name?" She was slightly taken aback by his knowledge of her name without her having to introduce herself.

"Well, I could walk on two from birth. And, about that…" He scratched his head, hesitant about revealing his powers. He explained in detail that by using his shapeshifting abilities to transform into objects or beings, he could share thoughts, memories, and behaviours, including how to talk like them and the name of the being he transforms into.

She found it a little creepy, but she was still brimming with questions, asking about the origin of his name. Hades explained that he was named as 'Hades, the Unseen One' as he eluded the eyes of the Hunters who wanted to capture him for the intergalactic black market. Casey later added that his name was the name of one of the deities of the underworld in legends, adding that it seemed quite fitting for him as foxes like him would stay in dens underground which was literally 'under the world'.

"You know, walking and talking animals would be kinda silly on Earth as they don't really… exist, unless it's a cartoon or movie for children." She thought of Hades as a figment of somebody's imagination, like some of the animated characters she had seen before. "But as for your case, you're like a sort of magical creature with your weird, whacky powers."

"Well, I guess I'm kinda magical if you put it in that way. I'm gifted with Empyrean magic for shapeshifting, but that's all for the magic I have inside of me," he said patting his stomach jokingly, which caused her to giggle a small bit.

Afterwards, he proceeded to share briefly about his friends who had also been given powers of a similar spectrum to his, especially Leo whom he would look up to as a leader, often calling him "Foxy" as a nickname.

"Coincidentally, that's what I wanted to name you, but, I guess it's alright."

"It's supposed to be a one-off joke that I'm his pet, but he still treats me like that throughout the whole journey we shared together. I feel that I have more sentience than being one and I dislike it when someone like I'm a pet or something."

"No offence, Hades, but on Earth, anything with fur, paws and a tail, following a human is counted as a pet under any human's perception. Well, go on."

With a sigh, he continued rambling on about his past adventures with Leo. In the span of the next few minutes, he recounted the journey through the galaxy from planet to planet trying to find the other Empyreans before finally defeating a great evil who threatened to take over his galaxy. He eventually got to the point where he told her about how he was trapped in an explosion and ended up on Earth, still stuck.

While he continued about how he was being chased, he began fiddling with different items in the room as he walked around. Examining different foreign items, he lifted each item to his eye level until something caught his attention. His voice ceased abruptly as soon as his eyes wandered towards the tin of cookies he sighted in front of him. It was a blue metallic tin with pictures of assorted butter cookies, some of them he could recognise as he savoured them before.

"Ooh! Cookies!" He said as he interrupted himself, holding the tin in front of him. "Can I have some?"

With a thumbs-up, Casey permitted him to have them, knowing that he might be hungry after having the whole slew of events happened. Almost immediately, he began engorging himself with the cookies, munching them loudly and consuming everything speedily.

"Hee hee. You're a sweet tooth, just like me," she chuckled.

"Mm-hmm!" He responded with his voice muffled by the cookies that filled his mouth.

Once he was finished with the remaining bulk of cookies, she suggested that they walked around the park close by to get some fresh air after having been in the room for a few hours.

As they reached the park, they were welcomed by a gush of invigorating breeze from the trees in the forest nearby, walking on the pavement of the path along the lake in the middle. However, the deeper they moved into the park, the more Hades suspected something was up.

"Hey Casey, I'm getting the feeling that someone or something is watching us," he said as he felt the fur on the back of his ears stand. "Also, I feel strange around these parts…"

She took a panoramic glance and she, too, found it weird as there were no one but them strolling on the path. Typically, there would be people fishing at the lake or jogging around, but there was only wind present. It was then they decided that they returned home immediately before anything happened.

Out of nowhere, a yellow beam of energy shot out from the bushes, causing Hades to leap up high in surprise and splash into the lake beside. He waded through the water with added effort as his fur was soaked to the skin, weighing him down as he trudged out.

"Brr!" He uttered as he tried to shake off all the water from his fur.

"What was that?" Casey asked, puzzled about why he leapt into the water out of the sudden. Before they could continue forward, they heard some loud rustling in the bushes around them.

To their horror, they could see several men in black suits and shades running towards them, quickly surrounding them in a few seconds. He gulped. He turned to her and saw a confused look on her face, observing their problems arising apace. He whispered into her ears and informed her that those were the assailants chasing him from the start right after he arrived on Earth. On realisation, her eyes widened as she became immediately unsettled.

"You're cornered you little rascal! You thought we left the park, didn't you?" They demanded as they pointed pistols and tranquiliser guns in their direction. "Both of you, come with us or you'll get hurt!"

"How about no?" He declined defensively without hesitation, standing in front of Casey with his arms outstretched. Hoping that something would happen out of a miracle, he converged his paws together, accidentally casting a shockwave spell which threw the assailants backwards onto their rears. His spell deflected their bullets away from them and the tranquillizer beams right back at them, stunning them momentarily, providing them with some time to escape.

'Phew! Thank the heavens that Empyrea is watching over me. I'm glad I'm still able to use Leo's powers. That'll be useful in the future,' he thought as stared at his paws upon discovering that he could still use Leo's power, even if he could not transform into him.

Using his imitative powers of Leo again, he wiped out their memories of them right, running as fast as their legs could carry out of the park afterwards. Throughout the journey back, they were vigilant of surroundings and ensured that they did not follow them, finally returning home without any additional problems.

Upon returning to Casey's home, she hastily closed the curtains and locked the doors to prevent anyone from discovering Hades. She sat down on the couch, still somewhat breathless from running.

"Whew! That's a close one," she heaved a sigh of relief while she wiped off the sweat from her forehead. "Hades, it seems those people chasing you aren't just normal assailants. From the looks of it, they seem like the special forces who collect extraterrestrial remains or imprison aliens or for experimentation from science fiction movies. The alien is pretty much... *you*, no doubt about it."

He turned speechless when she mouthed the word and pointed directly to his snout. Being curious as he was, Hades transformed into one of them in a split second, absorbing all the knowledge and learning everything about who those people were. His temporary transformation into one of them terrified Casey, causing her to jump out of her skin and slowly inched away from him on the couch. Once he reverted to his true form, his eyes widened in surprise when he turned towards her.

"Hey, Casey, you were right! From the memories of one of them, they do deal with aliens, more specifically, aliens with a certain level of sentience!" he exclaimed, unable to explain any of the details himself, baffled by the things he saw through his assailant's memories. "These people are the agents of a secret group called SAIRO, the Scientific Association of Intelligent Race and Organisms."

"Well, now we know. The walls have ears, the streets have eyes, it's just how it is here in America."

He tilted his head to the side, raising an eyebrow as he was unsure of what he meant.

"Does it have a tail too?"

"No, it's just a figure of speech, Hades. These people are watching us from every corner ever so closely since you're like a magnet for attention. We'll need to be careful in the future and you'll need to disguise yourself with your shapeshifting powers if you wanna appear in public again."

As the hours passed, it eventually became night again. Casey yawned while she sat at her bed, offering Hades to sleep with her patting at her bed invitingly. However, he preferred to rest on the tree outside her window, longing to stay in the covers of leaves as he did before in his original home.

While lying down, she watched him, perched on the tree branch and getting himself in a comfortable spot by resting his head and body against the barks. Once settled, he was watching the skies and staring vacantly at the stars, seemingly downcast as his ears slowly drooped backwards.

"Is there someone you miss, Hades?"

He turned to her and nodded as he sniffled slightly, attempting to retrain his tears and hiding emotions from her, whilst ailing for home.

"I miss my friends, all of them somewhere out there worrying about me, especially Leo. I wonder if..." His voice began to trail off as he dozed off into a deep subconscious state, his mouth wide open with his tongue sticking out to the edge, leaving his paws hanging by the side of the branch. Admiring the position of how he slept, she too, allowed her eyelids to slowly shut, awaiting a new day's surprise.

Deep in his subconsciousness, Hades was situated in a dark void, silent until a bright light flare lit up the darkness, revealing Empyrea as the glare gradually turned dim.

"How are you holding in the new world?"

"The trip here is a bit rough, but I'm kinda lost here and there without Leo. He's always been a leader to decide how I do things."

"Hades, you proved that you could be self-sufficient for the time you've been here, even without him. Unfortunately, you're separated from him by inordinate margins. To put it another way, it's very difficult for you to return home unless certain conditions are satisfied. If you wish to reunite with him once more, you'll need to retrieve the Shard to open a temporary gateway to him, as he shall do the same at a particular point in time which will be known to you soon. However, any failure to synchronise the two sides will lead to permanent, inconceivable anomalies which might render your existence null. Staying in this world is dangerous for your very being, which also means your time is limited here."

Hades gasped. "But-"

"Yes. I know they've taken it," she voiced out right before he tried to reason with her. "The next few months will be an arduous struggle, both physically and emotionally, but don't give in. And, I foresee something big coming your way in the future, darkness created by the very essence of light, unknown yet familiar. Be wary."

As he was woken by the time Empyrea finished what she had to say, he mumbled to himself, "what a weird dream. I wonder if it's trying to tell me something important."

"It is," a voice followed by a sigh echoed in his head.

With a small giggle to kick-start the day, he anticipated that everything would go smoothly from then on, even if she had said otherwise.

But would it really?

Chapter 3

(The Sanctuary)

As the morning grew late, Hades pounced onto the bed, bouncing Casey out of her sweet slumber.

"Urgh! It's the weekends, Hades. Lemme sleep for a bit longer..." She groaned, turning to the other side of the bed. Being cheeky as he was, he positioned his snout close to her face on the bed and gave her puppy-dog-eyes. On his every breath, she could feel the warm "breeze" caress her face, eventually opening her eyes, only to be staring eye to eye at him.

"Alright, alright. I'm awake." She sat up with her hair messy and flying all about, and she was still groggy from waking up. "Gimme a minute to change and we'll get going."

After getting changed out of her pyjamas and tidying up her appearance, she proposed an idea that he would come along to visit her father's wildlife sanctuary. It was where many injured animals were rescued, and most importantly, where he was treated before he stayed with her. However, in order for him to come along, Casey needed him to do one more thing.

"Well, if you're tagging along, you'll need a disguise through your shapeshifting powers to look like one of the foxy counterparts in the sanctuary if you're to appear close to other people," she said as she lifted up a map of the sanctuary, pointing towards a picture of a red fox. "And once we're there, don't talk and just act like one of the other foxes. I don't want you attracting too much unwanted attention, much less, those pesky agents again."

He twitched his ears and scratched the back of his head, remembering Amber the fox to replicate her looks. Without much effort on his powers, he finally transformed into a quadrupedal red fox, one that seemed ordinary. Oblivious to Casey's next move, he turned to her, only to see her hands raising a bright red bandana towards his neck. He was staring in dismay as one of his worst nightmares was coming true right in front of him - being treated like a pet.

"One last finishing touch for a snazzy little fella?" She grinned with an intense smile as he was backed into the corner of the bed. Without any suitable paths to escape his "predicament", he gave in to what was about to come.

In a few rapid successions of folds and a knot, he had a red bandana draped around his neck. He sighed and uttered a long line of complaints under his breath as he obliged, mortified and feeling that this was somewhat demeaning.

After a short drive, they returned to the sanctuary to visit Casey's father at work, watching and "assisting" as they spent their time there. But just watching her father treat animals was getting boring for him, so he decided to move about the sanctuary in his disguised form.

During the break times, while no one was around, Hades would wander around on all fours to visit other sanctuaries to communicate with the animals inside, gradually getting to know them and their backgrounds before they were rescued to stay there. Slowly, he revealed his true form to them, letting their fears of seeing him subside and convincing them that he was friendly.

Soon, the other animals became acquainted with having him around as a unique creature, walking around in his true form every now and then when there were no visitors present in the sanctuary. On the weekdays, while Casey was busy in school, he would follow her father to the sanctuary, playing about and chatting with the resident animals there, giving him a sort of entertainment to chase his boredom away.

When the sanctuary was open, people from all walks of life would come to visit. At times, he would interact with these visitors in various interesting ways. He would lead visitors around each enclosure, putting a paw on each sign placed to allow them to get an introduction to know the animals who resided in every enclosure better.

And soon, he was becoming a popular "celebrity" around the sanctuary, eventually becoming the mascot of the sanctuary known as the "Little Foxy Helper".

Months passed without a hitch as Hades spent his time at the sanctuary during the weekdays. On the weekends, both he and Casey helped injured animals return to the pink of health, either releasing them or letting them live in the sanctuary.

But throughout the days, Hades could always notice a recurring pattern. One of the visitors, who was always wearing shades and a black business suit, showed up every time he was present and stared at him intently every time he passed through. Assuming that it was a normal habit of some visitors to eye on him so closely, he continued ignoring it as he thought of himself as an attraction.

One day, as Hades was taking a break, he sighted someone familiar. It was the red fox he met in the pine forest on the day he arrived. He went to her side and asked, "Amber, do you recognise me?"

"No, but your voice sure sounds oddly familiar," she said in her foxy shrills.

"I'm Hades, the purple walking fox you saw in the whitebark forests," he transformed to reveal his true form for a second before he hid under his alter ego again.

"It's nice to see that you're still well after a couple of months. I couldn't recognise you with your disguise. Your human friend over there seemed nice too. But…" She then sighed and dipped her snout down, her mind bogged down by something. Being concerned, he asked what was bothering her.

She then recalled a few days ago, she was captured by some people dressed in black pinned her down and caged her. In captivity, she was experimented on, scanned for any alien traces or foreign contaminants. As time went on, she recalled overhearing them talking about some purple alien, whom she assumed was Hades.

"Yep! Sounds a lot like me, alright!"

"It's you, dummy! That's my worry," she said as she prodded his snout gently with her paw. "And so…"

As she resumed her story, she mentioned that she was released in a few hours. However, one of them, wearing shades and donned in brown, kicked her down a hill in annoyance after learning that I was not what they wanted, leaving her tumbling down on the rocky face of the hill. At the bottom of the hill, she had been bruised and hurt, unable to walk due to the overwhelming agony in her hind legs. She howled for help for hours on end and was eventually rescued by hikers who then brought her to the sanctuary.

After hearing her story, he pondered for a moment, realising what that meant to him. That was the same man who stared at him every time he visited. He was in certain danger, knowing that the man visited the sanctuary often. But as the man in shades was not around, he decided he would take a break instead of worrying too much about him.

When he was finished with a bit of chatter to catch up, Hades went to the external garden to enjoy the cool breeze and relax, lying on top of a marble ledge, dawdling his time away.

Suddenly, he sneezed and his ears twitched harder than it ever before, giving him an acute sting of pain as he heard the screams of his name echoing in his head. "Hmm… Strange, I could have sworn I heard Leo voice calling me for a second, but I'm not sure how or why. It's like he's warning me of danger or something…" He murmured to himself while he rubbed his snout with his paws, sniffling a little from his sneeze.

"Trust your instincts, Hades. Your instincts are always right."

"Empyrea?" He tried to talk to her, but there was only silence after her forewarning. And before he knew it, he closed his eyes and had a premonition of the agents surrounding the building, equipped with tranquiliser guns and pistols. Before the end of his vision, he saw himself in some sort of dimly-lit room of sorts that he could not recognise.

"They are coming! Run!" Empyrea's voice rang in his head like an alarm while the visions played out, a warning with utmost urgency. With the given knowledge of the situation, he scurried towards Casey and alerted her by tugging on her jeans. She knelt down and picked him up, moving to a more obscure spot of the veterinarian clinic to chat with him.

Once every word was relayed to her, she carried him in her arms and bolted towards the front door, but it was too late. She had bumped into a pistol-wielding SAIRO agent who blocked her path, threatening her to stay inside. She knew that they were trapped, stepping back into the middle of the room with Hades in her arms.

"Surround the building! Make sure no one and nothing enters or leaves the vicinity!" he commanded over his handheld radio. Turning back to look at her, he raised his pistol yet again and pointed it towards her forehead. "And as for you, we know that you're hiding the purple alien. Hand it over or you'll be in big trouble, little girl."

Being petrified by anxiety, she felt numbness in every limb she had, finding difficulty in moving her lips to answer. Leaving them with no way to escape, Hades decided it would be easier to surrender and spare the trouble or endangerment of his friends. He hopped off Casey's arms and shapeshifted back to his purple self, revealing his true form in front of the agents.

"Please don't hurt anyone. If you're looking for me, take me and leave the sanctuary and my friends alone," he said as raised both his paws up.

"But…"

Hades reassured her it would be safe, placing a paw on her shoulder with a faint smile.

"Hades, you didn't have to do this…" She protested resentfully under her breath.

And without any further delay, he was shot in the gut with the beam of the tranquiliser gun, leaving him limp in the hands of the agent as they took him away. As he took a last glimpse before he fainted, he saw Casey's eyes full of tears, collapsing down onto the floor in sadness. He too shed a stream of tears, his eyes forced shut by the potent narcotic effects of the beam.

Chapter 4

(The Clone)

While he was unconscious, the SAIRO agents took him down into their secret facility deep underground.

As he awoke, he discovered that he was in some sort of alien confinement cell. It was spacious, but he still felt trapped, although he was not strapped nor tied down to anything. At the roof of his cell was a bright fluorescent strip of light. Along the walls were several rusted pipelines running across the cell, each having several holes being drilled into it. The holes seem peculiar to him, with a knowledge that pipes should not have holes otherwise they would leak, unless they were suspiciously drilled for another hidden purpose.

Shrugging away his thoughts of what the holes were, he moved to one side of the cell to view his surroundings through the glass pane. He sighted several SAIRO scientists in gloves and lab coats moving about with brown clipboards while they pressed buttons from other cells, progressively stepping closer towards him.

"Specimen IR-14 requires a cloned copy for experimentation and autopsy. We cannot lose this specimen to any kind of test. It's our one, and only, alive subject from Site 43, unlike the others who are expendable. This one, from the way he looks at us, has a high level of sentience," one of them conveyed his plans as he looked intently at Hades.

"Now, why did you come to Earth, purple one? Do you have any purpose here?"

"I-I have no idea how I even got here. I don't have anything planned here," he replied nervously.

"Stop lying!" He demanded, as he shook his head in disappointment and banged against the glass with his fist. "Seems like we can only get answers from the experimentations since you want to make it so difficult!"

"Prepare IR-14 for cloning!" And with the command, they all gazed at him for a moment before they pressed a button on a control panel, causing sleeping gas to be piped into the cell. Visible greenish gas seeped into the cell through the holes of the pipe, slowly filling up the cell to the brim, causing him to breathe in and choke on the noxious gasses. It was torture as he tried to cough out the gas, holding on to his consciousness with all his effort. But to no avail, with every exhale, he was making himself breathe in more of it as he gasped for air. And soon, his mind went blank as he fainted.

Before Hades knew what was going on, he was woken from his unconscious state, colliding his head into the glass wall as he sat up. He uttered a yelp of pain, shaking his fur back to its neat condition and blinking several times to see where he was currently at more clearly. Through observation of his surroundings, he was placed into a much smaller, brightly-lighted, cylindrical chamber with wires attached above and below, linking up to a convoluted machine that had different coloured indication lights flickering on and off. Alongside his chamber was another chamber like his, but it was dark and unlit, not to mention that it was empty.

Upon noticing that Hades was awake, the scientists rushed to prepare everything on their checklist. With all the inspections and preparations done, one of them flipped a switch and the light in his chamber glowed with a yellow hue. While the process was ongoing, nothing happened to both chambers, leaving the scientist with no visible or tangible results.

After a few more minutes of futile attempts, they decided in a general consensus to check on the machine's settings and blueprints to reconfigure it.

"We need more power! Something isn't quite right with the process!" Someone shouted from the other corner of the room. As Hades watched the scientists move around in a frenzy like ants trying to solve their errors, he heard the voices of two scientists beside him, discussing something unclear with differing facial expressions which invoked his curiosity.

Pressing his right ear against the glass, he began eavesdropping on their private conversations, giving him more information on what they were going to do next. While they spoke, they mentioned something about the mysterious glowing crystal found in the "crash site" of what they thought was a UFO. They concluded that the cloning process for him required another different type of energy source apart from electricity, which was the role of the "energy stone" that they found at the site.

He watched the two of them leave the laboratory, returning with a type of metallic energy canister with the Shard held in place by metallic supports and wires. Next, they attached it to the cloning machine via the wires and used it as an alternative power source. As they switched on the machine again, Hades could feel a strange tingling sensation around his body. Both he and the Shard started to glow as the energy that resonated between the two was siphoned into the empty chamber.

He attempted to break the glass of the chamber with his Empyrean abilities, but none of them worked. The glass was charged with a strong electromagnetic field, interfering with his ability to use his powers and in turn thwarting his escape plan.

Gradually, he felt his body's stamina constantly drain away as the process continued and he needed to do something to escape the chamber. He began protesting and banged repeatedly on the glass, but only muffled screams escaped the confines of the small chamber.

While he was successful at getting the scientists' attention, he infuriated them, ruining their train of thought and concentration.

"Shut this vicious beast up! I can't think with all that racket!" And with that instruction, they shocked him with electricity on the press of a button, causing Hades to feel all his limbs convulsing, slumping backwards onto the floor of the chamber in agony. Although he was paralysed by the electrical shock, he was still able to view the empty chamber in his current slumped position.

Soon, the empty chamber began to illuminate with a blue glimmer, eventually releasing a burst of blinding light. Amidst all the brightness, a shadowy outline of what seemed to be a copy of him was being conjured out of his Empyrean energy. As it began taking shape, the scientists were busy viewing the overloading energy gauges and recording everything that took place. Soon, the gauges exploded and strewn shards of glass everywhere, missing the scientists gathered around the contraption by an inch.

"IR-15 is a success!" They cheered, tossing all the items in their hands up in the air and congratulating each other of their accomplishments. While the light emitted from the other chamber died down, Hades' eyes began to close as the wave of exhaustion hit him after getting all his energy depleted from his body.

When he awoke once more, he realised that he was back in the alien confinement cell, but this time, he was with his clone who was still unconscious, lying next to where he lay. He thought that it was amazing to see a doppelganger, a spitting image of himself. Like him, it was magenta, just a slightly faded hue from the colour his fur. It had a metallic dog tag encircling its neck, the shine of the metallic chain glinting through its fur.

As he put his paw around his chest, he discovered that he had it too, something he did not notice until now. Inspecting his tag, he read it to himself softly, "Hmm... IR-14, Intelligent Race - Experiment 14. I guess I could take that as a compliment."

From afar, he could not make out any of the letterings on his clone's dog tag as the tufts of its fur covered it. He was curious to read it and proceeded to walk towards his clone. Just when he attempted to read his double's dog tag, he noticed a slight flicker of the lights before the whole lab plunged into pitch darkness. As the electromagnetic field around the cell was deactivated, his grasp of power slowly returned to him, allowing him to see through the darkness with ease.

Clasping this window of opportunity, he carried his clone in his arms and teleported out of the chamber onto the floor of the laboratory. However, he was unable to teleport any further due to the insufficient Empyrean energy in his body, leaving him no choice but to manually escape the facility on foot. Sighting an open vent in his path, he brought the clone in his arms through the vent into the air ducts.

As the ducts were too small for him to hold his clone in his arms, he carried it on his back, crawling to a blind spot where they could not be discovered. He took this moment to read his clone's dog tag. It was labelled "IR-15" and there was nothing else interesting about it, except when he turned to read the other side. "Specimen is expandable. Use whatever it takes to learn about them and their purpose, even if it leads to their demise - SAIRO."

Upon reading the horrific instructions on that side of the dog tag, he was glad that he could rescue his clone in time. Looking over his shoulder at his clone sleeping soundly, he could see all the features similar to his, from its snout to the tufts of fur on its head and chest. He continued down the ducts until it widened up, giving him ample space to stand up and carry it in his paws.

As time and stamina were running out while he carried his clone's weight, heaving to catch his breath from exhaustion. He felt that he had no choice but to wake his clone up for it to walk along with him. He placed his clone in his paws and shook it gently by its shoulders. After a few shakes, its eyelids began to open as it stirred from its sleep, staring back at him with a seemingly unending gaze from its purple eyes. Surprised, it nimbly hopped off his paws and stood up in front of him, its ears shifting backwards in fear.

"W-who are you?" She asked hesitantly, stepping backwards a little.

"Hello, I'm Hades. What's your- Oh..." On realisation he paused for a bit. "You'll need a name. How about... Iris? The name you were supposedly given looks like it spells out Iris," he suggested, naming her after both her dog tag and her purple eyes. She lifted the front side of her dog tag to her eyes and read, pondering for a while.

"Hmm? I like it!" She exclaimed in excitement, oblivious to the situation at the moment.

"Shhh! We need to be quiet. We're trying to escape now."

She gasped and covered her snout with her two paws in embarrassment.

"We'll need to move fast. Once the power is back on and they find out we're missing, all hell will break loose and they will scramble everywhere to find us."

Nodding in acknowledgement, they walked through the air ducts, with their footsteps on the metallic surface only audible to them. Being afraid, Iris held Hades by his paw, holding him to feel comforted that she was not alone. While they went through the labyrinth of tunnels, Hades shared more information about her being a clone created from his powers and explained most of the things that he saw happen while he was conscious.

As they pressed on further, they could feel a gentle breeze seeping through. Hades began sniffing the air, leaving his snout to point the way around the ducts. They were close to freedom.

On exiting the long meandering tunnels which felt like an eternity to navigate through, they found themselves in a grassy plain area which was devoid of any life or even signs of life.

"Hmph," Iris uttered, primping her fur as she brushed off the dust from the air ducts.

"Well, that's a whole mess we've escaped from."

"Uh-huh. Honestly, I've been through worse," Hades remarked, staring at the dog tag he lifted up from his body in his paws. "Let's take these off first."

Both of them removed their dog tags hanging from their necks and tossed them into the grass, leaving them behind to be forgotten.

"So now what?" Iris questioned, scratching the back of her head with an ear twitch.

"For now, our best bet for safety is to travel towards Casey's house. Since we share memories, you should know where it is."

However, as Hades was deprived of his powers, he was unable to warp both of them directly into her house. Iris, who was still fresh and brimming with Empyrean energy, suggested that she would teleport them instead, saving them time from walking all the way back on foot. As she prepared for the teleport, she drew a circle in the ground around them with magic, holding Hades by his paws before they zapped through the air and they were transported back into Casey's bedroom right above her bed, but fall was momentarily paused as they froze midair for a few seconds.

Once they landed from the air, the force of their fall startled Casey off her bed onto the ground beside.

"Hades! You're back!" She exclaimed and sighed in relief as she climbed back up onto her bed having woken up suddenly from the surprise that presented itself in front of her. "Wait a sec, who's that beside you?"

Hades elucidated every detail he could recall about Iris being a cloned copy of him and how close she was to being made into an experimental test subject in his place. He further retold his experience that they escaped together through a fortuitous blackout from the SAIRO laboratories.

After retelling the story, Iris wanted to have a breather from the frightful experience they had in the laboratory. Casey then suggested that both of them should hang out in the garden in the backyard to relax for the rest of the day. Leaving them to have fun by themselves, the duo stepped out into the garden in the backyard where whiffs fresh air entered their snouts.

At the garden, they capered around for a bit until the sky turned orange, the sun sinking bit by bit into the horizon. Both Hades and Iris sat on the swings attached to the tree, swaying to and fro while their legs flew about.

"Hades?"

"Yeah?"

"I-I feel like I was created for no specific purpose..." she said with downcast eyes, staring at her legs and shifting the sandy grounds below her feet as she gradually slowed down to a halt. When she stopped swinging, she began thinking that her life was bereft of any goals in mind.

"Hey Iris, that's not true. Like what Empyrea said to me before, everyone and everything has its purpose to fulfil, no matter how big or small its significance. You'll just need to discover it somehow.

You share my memories, why don't you seek through my memories for some examples?"

She tilted her head up to gaze at the starlit skies with a paw on her chin, pondering a bit to rethink her existence, rummaging through Hades' shared memories of his previous adventure. From one memory to the next, she could feel the warmth of purpose that was instilled in each, turning her frown into a simper.

Soon, the night had fallen upon them and Hades led her up the tree, clambering up together onto Hades' favourite tree branch to stargaze together. They watched the skies as the stars sparkled and eventually, a shooting star whizzed past over their heads.

"Make a wish Iris!" He exclaimed in excitement, raising his paw to point at the sky, turning his snout into Iris' direction.

"I-I wish... I wish for a bright future, w-where I live with a purpose to make those around me happy."

With a hug from Hades, they smiled as they slept in each others' embrace, envisioning their aspirations in the future ahead. From her bed, Casey watched them in silence from a distance, seeing them appear as though it was a scene from a romantic movie. She was elated for them to be so close to each other.

The next morning, they returned to Casey's room and laid beside her, one on each side of her ear, whispering "good morning" into both of them at once. This made her jump out of her skin before a relieved sigh, seeing that it was only them. She wrapped her arms around them and brought them close for a moment of huddles before eventually getting up.

As soon as she changed out of her pyjamas, they could hear that someone causing a raucous below with their thunderous knocking at the door. It was a constant triplet of thumps every few seconds, which would be able to wake anyone up, even on the upper floors of the house. Casey waited for her father to attend to the visitor as a habit of hers, but she realised that he was already busy working at the sanctuary by this time of the day.

"Argh! Who could that be at 10 am on a Sunday? You two should stay here just in case."

She stormed downstairs towards the front door to view through the peephole to see who it was. The moment she realised who it was, she tiptoed hastily back into her room, notifying them that it was the SAIRO agents which she could identify from the logos on their collars. They had threatening looks plastered all over their faces, holding up their weapons to prepare to enter.

The foxy duo needed to be concealed as soon as they could, but they were flustered as every hiding spot was too easily accessible if the SAIRO agents searched through the entire room. Even if they transformed into something, they would be easily identified as objects that were out of place. Hades in a state of frenzy, leaping up and down with his paws cupped at the sides of his head. While scuttling about the room to find an inconspicuous spot, Casey snapped her fingers and thought of a possible one.

"I know where you can be hidden! Quick, follow me!"

She slid open a stuffed-animal closet and asked them to transform into one of the various toys to blend in, minimising their chances of being discovered. Once they had transformed into two imitations and wiggled into position, she swiftly slid the closet close and proceeded to let the agents in.

As the agents were invited through the door, they demanded to know where the aliens were, knowing that she was formerly close to one the aliens. After searching around the living room and kitchen areas, they decided to take a look upstairs, making their way up to Casey's room

Casey, while following them, saw their sudden change in directions and ran up to her room, positioning herself in front of her closet. She was hoping to block anyone from a direct search.

"Little girl, alien concealment is a violation against the government and its secrets. If anything is found in your house, you'll be severely punished. Now if you excuse us, we're carrying out an investigation!"

"You've already taken away my only companion! I'm telling you. It's not here! No one is at home, except me!"

Ignoring her objections and protests they shoved her along and began searching every spot in her room where they could be hidden. Eventually, they came towards her to search her closet, one of the few spots that were not investigated by them yet.

"Move aside!" One of the demanded as she was blocking their path.

"I assure you, they're not here. This is my private collection of stuffed animals. I'll show you if you don't believe me!"

She then slid open the closet, revealing a huge pile of stuff toys and shifted them around to show them that there was nothing there, attempting to redirect their attention to other spots. "See?"

Still not fully convinced, they probed around the closet, causing both Hades and Iris to squirm slightly, holding back their giggles as they were poked by the agents' fingers. After a few minutes of futile searches in her room, they found nothing of extraneous origin and left empty-handed. Casey happily escorted them out of the house, swiftly showing them the way to the front door.

"Good day, my sirs!" She spurted out before she slammed the front door in their faces with a loud bang. "Whew! That felt good! I should really try that more often!"

Returning to check on the foxy duo, she saw that they had already transformed back by the time she returned, standing amidst the tumbling stack of soft toys.

"Phew!" Both heaved a sigh of relief in unison as they wiped their foreheads with their nervously trembling paws. Afterwards, Casey lifted them out of the heap of toys and kept the toys back inside the closet.

"That was a close one. I wouldn't wanna get caught by them again," Hades remarked as he clasped his chest as his heart was palpitating, still nervous from the visit from the agents.

"I guess you two should really stay inside the house from now on. You've got a high price on your heads," Casey advised, suggesting that they could play board games indoors or watch the television, minimising the probability that they would get caught.

Both Hades and Iris stared at each other, thinking of various ways to entertain themselves for the time being.

Chapter 5

(De-energized)

Days turned into weeks and both Hades and Iris were gradually getting overwhelmed with boredom from staying confined within the borders of the house. While they were burning away their days at home, something peculiar happened. As they were wandering around the house, Hades sighed and stopped where he stood, scratching the fur on his rear, yawning openly in the middle of the room. "Feels like being stranded in Xenia and not being able to do anything interesting all over again…"

"I feel you," Iris added, "both figuratively and literally", lying on the couch leaning her head against her paw. She turned to Hades and stood up, walking towards him to find something else to do together.

"Technically, you're me, so…"

As Iris tried to reply mischievously in a snarky fashion, she collapsed and fell limp on the ground of the living room, her eyes were forcefully shut as she felt a rush of agony disseminating throughout her body. She was wincing in pain, lying on her side and curled up into a ball.

"Iris?" He turned to look at her, only noticing her condition now. "Iris! Are you okay?"

She was so frail that she could only utter feeble yelps, unable to talk properly anymore. His intuition kicked in, giving him a rush of adrenaline to find Casey, dashing towards the garden outside at the back of the house. Grabbing her wrist with both his paws for attention, he pulled her into the house. She was horrified at the scene that beheld in front of her.

"Oh no..."

Without further ado, she ran over to inspect Iris and saw that there was a slight discolouration of her fur. Her breathing was turning heavy amidst the agony. Surrounding her was a dim violet aura, pulsating around like an intangible bubble of light. Being experienced in observing certain behaviours of sick animals she had seen at the sanctuary through working alongside her father, she knew that this was neither a normal sickness nor was it an injury.

"It seems like it's magic-related or something of some sort. I don't think anyone on earth would be able to help her, not even a professional wildlife vet like my father."

"But, what should we do then?" He said with both paws on his head, beginning to panic for a viable solution.

Without any ideas of how they could help Iris, they gave irresolute looks at each other as they sat down on the ground beside her. Previously, when things went rough, Leo would guide Hades and tell him what was the next plan of action to take. For him now, without Leo's leadership, he felt lost and felt that his thoughts went astray.

Just when they felt that their hopes of saving Iris were all lost, someone knocked on the front door. Casey moved over to the door to check on who it was through the peephole and she felt unsettled as soon as she saw a man dressed in a white lab coat and shades. His hair was gelled thoroughly and on his wrist was a strange watch-like device with darkened glass, something that looked as if it was fished out from fiction.

Shakily, her hand reached for the door and she opened it, he was standing silently at the doorstep with raised eyebrows, preparing himself to enter. With a gasp, Hades shouted, "he's part of SAIRO! Close the door!"

Immediately, she attempted to close the door in his face but he quickly stopped the door with his hand and foot.

"I know what you're thinking, but I do not mean any harm. Please let me explain everything. I'm here to help," he assured in his calming voice, easing the tensing situation they had at hand.

She eventually released the door after a bit of struggling, her stamina giving up on her as her strength was outmatched. Next, he then proceeded to sit on the couch and began introducing himself as Doctor Maverick, an undercover agent who worked alongside the SAIRO agents so that he could disclose some of their secrets to the authorities. Through SAIRO's catalogues of blueprints and research data, he knew that Iris was dying and came just in time to prevent that from happening, suggesting that they brought her to his laboratory to recover.

She was unsure of whether she could trust him or not. 'A strange man in shades popping out of nowhere with a proposition of a miraculous solution to the problem at hand is kinda suspicious. It seems like an elaborate plan for a trap, but I don't think we have any other choice,' she thought, desperate to do anything to save Iris. "Could you really help her?"

"Ah yes... Finally, a new specimen for me to work with- Ahem!" He muttered under his breath before clearing his throat right at the moment he was caught off guard by Casey's question.

"I'm sorry, what was that?"

"Th-that was... That was nothing! I was thinking about my formulations aloud. Sorry, I tend to get lost in thought from time to time," he replied anxiously, trying not to reveal his true intentions. "Anyway, this, as SAIRO calls it, is the case of Progressive Energetic Destabilization. The atoms in her body are not stable and therefore slowly breaking down into the same energy used to create her."

He further elaborated that since her body was not created with biogenetic components and chemicals, or simply physical make-up, her physical form was slowly disappearing. Without a re-energization process, she would diffuse into energy all around into non-existence with no trace left behind once she is fully discharged. "That is why she needs to recharge at my lab in order to stabilize her body to prevent her disappearance."

"One more question before we go! How did you find ever us, Maverick?"

"Well, I went through SAIRO's records on where you live after that visit to your home a few weeks ago. Luckily, I located you just in time using her estimated de-energization rate to find out when she needed help. Follow me."

With Iris brought in Casey's arms and Hades walking alongside her, they were escorted into a black car with darkened windows. They entered the car and saw that the windows were only see-through from the inside, preventing anyone from outside from peeking inside. She gulped as the doors closed, anxious about what was to come for them.

On the journey towards his laboratory, they noticed that the houses around them began disappearing the further they went, gradually exiting the small town into its outskirts until they reached a hill in the middle of a remote desert. After leaving the car, Maverick brought them to a weather-beaten reinforced metallic door, likely made to keep whatever outside out. Or, for containing whatever secrets which resided in the depths of the facility securely.

Casey could recognise it as one of the secret, highly-secured military facilities she would always see in sci-fi movies, a military bunker to be exact. But by the appearance of the rusted doors and peeling moss-green paint, she knew that it had long been abandoned or insufficiently maintained. Maverick raised his wrist with the unknown silvery watch device and held it in front of the door, illuminating the darkened glass portion of his device and causing the door to slide down vertically. The door opened up into a passageway with a deep metallic rumble.

As he invited them inside, Hades began to feel that something was indeed askew about the scientist. He could feel strange tingling down to his tail, which was the same sensation he felt when one of the SAIRO agents chased him. The moment the door slammed shut behind him, it sent shivers throughout his body. There was no turning back now, he thought.

The passage eventually opened up into a brightly lit laboratory space where there were bubbling beakers and test tubes, liquid-filled chambers and a raised platform with a weird contraption, which Hades found to be familiar as it resembled the cloning chamber that Iris was previously placed in.

Next, Maverick took out a blue glowing stone from his lab coat, revealing it that he was the one who deliberately tripped a blackout at the SAIRO laboratories to take a charged energy stone away in order to save Iris. But, while he got the stone, she was already out of the laboratory and he could not save her then.

"Some charged stone, you say? Do you mean the Shard?" Hades pointed out, correcting him on its name.

"Yes, what you call 'the Shard' is needed to restore her body's stability, which I procured from SAIRO through laborious effort to hack into their interface to deactivate all their security systems. Put this anti-radiation collar around her neck just in case anything goes wrong and place her in the re-energization chamber," he said, unhitching the contraption doors to open it up.

As the collar was strapped around her neck, it was automatically activated and small lights began to flicker. Once she was positioned inside the chamber, Maverick hastily hooked up the wires and a smaller canister-shaped machine where he inserted the Shard in place. To his surprise, Hades could also recognise it as the same energy canister that was used as an energy extractor to clone him.

"Two of you, stand back behind within yellow safety circle. It's dangerous for both of you to stand so close and in the circle, there are special radiation-absorbing tiles to ensure your safety," he instructed, checking all the data displays and gauges, being pedantic to ensure that nothing could go wrong. Once they stepped behind the safety line, he looked at them and nodded, signifying the commencement of the process. He checked every step he took to initialise the chamber's powers by flipping switches systematically.

"Power has been set to a hundred percent, twenty and counting. Thirty, forty…"

They watch the chamber as it began to illuminate with a bluish shimmer, turning more intense in brightness as he voiced out each threshold of numbers. Hades sniffed the air for a moment before prodding Casey with his paw to get her attention.

"Something smells fishy around here, and I don't think it's only the lab that reeks of it," he whispered with a cupped paw, making sure that Maverick could not hear him. He recalled that in the Xenian laboratory he had been into with Leo in the past, it was a safety line, bordered out of the proximity of the dangerous contraptions, not just a circular area for them to stand in. He was also pretty sure that they were too close to the contraption presented in front of them for them to be safe.

When he voiced out that it was a hundred percent, he turned towards the left out of the sudden and flipped a yellow switch, causing a dome of bulletproof glass to fall around them, trapping them inside.

"Hey! What's all this? I thought you were helping us!" Hades banged on the glass, infuriated by the double-crossing at the last second.

"I was helping myself revive the experiment! For you two, I shall keep both of you in here forever, rotting away in the darkness. And with my new weapon, the IR-15, I shall show the world what I'm capable of, even the likes of SAIRO who thought my experiments were a pointless failure. It's time to move on to Phase Two of my plan to make my name known to the world as its new ruler!"

Without any delay, he whipped out a black remote control and grabbed the Shard from the canister. Hastily, he attached it to the remote and turned a knob, pointing it towards Iris with hypnotic energy targeted at her collar. In response, her body began to levitate and glow ominously. She broke out of the re-energization chamber explosively, scattering metal and glass shrapnel all over the room, with bits of it clattering against the glass dome. Maverick, on the other side of the room, protected himself with his force field he whipped up from his special wristwatch.

"And, now with the Shard, I can synchronise its energies with her brainwaves using the hypnosis collar and now, she's my puppet to control!" He finished off with a cackle as the beam was intensified, watching his plan come into fruition. As her eyes opened under the hypnotic beam, they appeared soulless with a faint white glow as her pupils constricted and eventually disappeared. Her emotions had been drained and her free will had vanished entirely under Maverick's control.

While she was being hypnotised, he unveiled what could only be described as a triangular spaceship with darkened windows from under a silvery-white blanket, floating naturally by itself. As the spaceship was powered up, they could see Iris floating alongside the ship. Soon, both of them zoomed out of the laboratory at great speeds, tearing a hole through the reinforced walls as if they were made of paper.

While they flew off, both Hades and Casey were stuck in the dusty laboratory, staring at both Iris and the spaceship as they gradually disappeared in the distance.

Chapter 6

(Chaos In the City)

Casey rummaged her backpack trying to find something that could help them escape but realised she had nothing to break this thickness of glass with. She only had a metallic thermos flask, a jacket and an extra set of clothes. Hades was the only one who could get them out of the trap, somehow or another.

Hades inspected the glass, tapping on it with his paws, leaning his ears against it to listen for the sounds of the vibration around the glass. On closer inspection, he discovered it was surrounded by a strong electromagnetic field, which did not allow him to teleport out through the glass.

He tried shapeshifting and using imitated abilities with his paw, realising that he still could use his powers to transform seeing that he could turn his arms orange. However, the abilities of those he shapeshifted into were significantly weakened. It was to an extent that even transforming into Leo was not able to make the cut for the sufficiency in power to break out, but he could only think of one being who could still do it even when drastically weakened.

"Hey Casey, I've got a crazy idea." And bit by bit, he relayed his idea of transforming into Empyrea, the most powerful being from his Universe. He had never tried to shapeshift into her even once in the past because he was restricted from doing so by the very being, but desperate times calls for desperate measures. "Empyrea, please allow me to transform into you this time."

He focused his mind on a memory of seeing Empyrea, visualizing her in mind to attempt to transform into her, but while he did, time stopped for a brief moment by cosmic means as Empyrea's voice echoed into his head, "Hades, upon transforming into me shall you learn the secrets of life and death and all the events of timelines which will eventually happen. Keep every piece of knowledge to yourself to prevent leading the path of spacetime astray, understood?"

Using his thoughts, he solemnly agreed to her and gradually transformed into a white spirit with two bulbous eyes and two purple markings above the eyes, along with a long and bushy white tail. Now with unlimited Empyrean energy in his grasp, he would be able to destroy the dome without breaking a sweat, even if his powers were diminished. Closing his eyes, he shifted his paws in front of him and waved them in a circular motion, intensely vibrating the glass dome until the dome turned into fine sand. Once they were free, Hades transformed back to his original self, he vigorously shook off bits of sand in his fur.

"Whew! That's some bit of a workout on my body," he remarked, panting from the intense usage of his powers, temporarily drained for the moment as it took a toll on his body. He fell back on his hind to rest for a while, wiping the sweat off his forehead.

Once he was adequately rested, he leapt up from the ground to stand and punched one of his paws up, pointing upwards. "Time to find Iris!"

"But how? They could be anywhere on the other side of the world at that kind of sci-fi speed!"

Tapping into his Empyrean ability to link his memory to Iris' via a telepathic connection, he traced her location through her vision and saw her in a city through her eyes, seeing all the chaos and devastation wrought by her very paws. Although he knew that she was in a city, he still could not identify exactly where she was.

The next thing he did was to consult Casey of the city he saw, placing a paw on her forehead for her to 'view' the cityscape of the location he had in mind. She closed her eyes and opened her eyes right away once she saw the cityscape, identifying the location as New York City. Unfortunately, it was too far an undertaking if they travelled on foot. And as for Hades, he was too unsure where to teleport to and even if he tried, it might bring them somewhere random.

"Why must villains always attack New York? That's so typical," she grumbled with a sigh, recognising it as a cliché from superhero movies which she had seen in the past.

Glancing around the room, he caught sight of another spaceship covered by a similar silvery blanket. Upon removal of the blanket, what he revealed from beneath was a metallic craft with a thick layer of dust which coated it like a layer of skin. Rubbing off some of the dust at a particular point on the outside of the ship, he was astonished by the sight which beheld him.

"Hey! A Xenian spaceship! I know how to fly this thing! C'mon Casey, let's find Iris!" He exclaimed in excitement as he saw the familiar-looking symbol of the Xenian Intergalactic Federation on the sides of the spaceship. He began pushing a set of tiles on the external skin of the ship like a keypad, opening up a hatch into a staircase leading inside, allowing them to climb up into the ship with ease.

From the outside, it appeared smaller and seemed congested on the inside of the ship. However, it was much more spacious than they had originally assumed. Unlike their assumptions, it had seats with a comfortable leg and adequate headroom. The seats were padded with cushions that felt like clouds as they laid back onto. Hades explained that this could be one of the private Xenian ships that came from the federation headquarters of Xenia made for long-haul hyperspace travel. Hence, it was designed to be capacious along with the high-quality of comfort inside the ship.

"So, how do you even know how to fly this thing?"

"Well, I retained the knowledge and thoughts of some of the greatest inventors of my Universe from shapeshifting into them. Trust me, if it's a Xenian ship, it's a breeze to fly with their wisdom. Strap in, we're taking off soon!"

While Casey secured herself to her seat, Hades quickly adjusted a few switches and knobs, and the ship bellowed to a start almost immediately. He checked the displays and sighted an energy detection radar which he could use to pinpoint Iris' exact location, travelling in the direction of New York City.

After a few minutes of streaking through the skies, they reached the city in the proximity of where the strong energy reading resonated from. As they flew closer to the where the surge of energy readings was, they were welcomed by a horrific sight.

Buildings were destroyed and vehicles were overturned in a wreck where Iris was. She was floating midair, her paws charged with energy, ready for more destruction. People ran away hysterically while Iris wrecked the city, fearing for their lives and trying to leave the vicinity as soon as possible. She flew around frenetically through the air while Maverick controlled her every move from his spaceship, silently hovering over her head.

When Hades and Casey arrived in their ship, Iris immediately shifted her eyes toward them and struck the ship with a jolt of intense energy. Before the ship exploded, Hades teleported both himself and Casey out of the ship to a close-by bus stop, staying low and hidden from the sights of Iris.

"Casey, I'll take care of her. Meanwhile, just take cover around here where she can't see you."

"Aight! Be careful, Hades."

Hades used the imitative form of Leo's magic, launching himself up into the air to look at Iris eye to eye.

"Iris!" As soon as he called for her, she turned her piercing gaze towards him, causing him to feel perturbed.

"Don't do this! This is not you!" He begged her to stop, shaking her by her shoulder to attempting to snap her out from her hypnosis. Her subservient pupils suggested otherwise as she unleashed a surge of energy towards him from behind her back. Instinctively, the fur on the back of his neck stood up just before she attacked, giving him forewarning of her every move, allowing him to teleport away before she even struck.

While he teleported from building to building, he avoided every attack she threw at him, closely missing his body as he dodged. Unfortunately, every "missed" attack contributed to the cumulative damage to the city as they flew, in which he was oblivious about. Turning to his shoulder to take a glimpse at Iris, he then thought of an ingenious idea. He could take away the remote control from Maverick to allow her to regain control of herself to stop this mess.

Speedily, he made an about-turn swerve towards Maverick's ship, attempting to break into his ship to snatch the remote. However, as he was closing in, Iris teleported in front of him and created a magical barrier, rebounding him away like a trampoline before he even touched the ship.

"Oh no, you don't!" She growled defensively.

Hades, in response, teleported around to try to outsmart her but after several failed attempts of repeatedly colliding into the magical barrier she cast, he felt that the only way to stop Maverick was through defeating Iris. While he was distracted by thought, she continued firing Empyrean energy spells at him, resuming the pursuit from before. As he weaved around the skyline of the city, Iris blasted through every single building that blocked her, destroying anything in the way of her mission to eliminate Hades.

Turning around and stopping mid-air with a paw raised towards her face. Seeing that he had gestured to stop, she levitated in front of him. Upon seeing the aftermath from the chase, Hades realised he had no choice but to retaliate instead of holding back to prevent the further destruction of the city. With the paw in front of him, he proceeded to cast a repulsive spell, blasting her a distance away from him.

He then travelled towards her and began his barrage of attacks, chasing her up into the sky to a height where damage to buildings was at a minimum while they fought. As their spells exploded through the clouds, it caused the clouds to shift, giving Hades some cover for a hidden attack he planned on executing.

He launched several "dud" spells to congregate the clouds into a white cloak for cover, hiding from her as she continued shooting energy spells in different directions. He waited until she stopped before teleporting in front of her and hurtling a fully-fledged burst of energy at her. With the pawful of energy sent whirling onto her body, she plunged towards the ground. However, before her body impacted the ground, he conjured up a magical bubble below her which cushioned the brunt of the force of her fall, saving her from certain death.

As her eyelids opened slightly, she could see Hades carrying her up in his paws, holding her with anxiety painted all over his face, concerned about her current wellbeing.

"Iris, do you remember me? Please, snap out of it, for our sake…"

She rubbed her eyes and blinked, trembling as she stood up to shake off the dust from her fur.

"I-I… I'm sorry about everything I've done. I don't know what's wrong with me," she cried, sniffling in her tears as she rubbed her eyes intermittently.

"It wasn't your fault, Iris," he consoled, trying to pry the straps of the hypnosis collar off vigorously with the nails of his paws. However, the collar seemed to be locked tightly, requiring him to use special alternative methods of removing it.

"Hades, I-I…"

But, before she could finish, Maverick's ship was above them and the glint from the glass of the hovering ship could be seen from below. He knew his window of opportunity to free Iris from her suffering was over, regretting not removing the collar first.

"What are you doing, IR-15? Attack!" He commanded, sending an intense beam of Empyrean energy towards her, dealing greater agony than before, causing her pupils to constrict and turned lifeless again. This time, she had a menacing crimson glare as the hypnotic beam clouded her judgement, her mind being controlled once more.

Without hesitation, Iris explosively moved her limbs and kicked Hades away before rising into the air to transform. He turned to see her and watched the terror unfold. She was flying up with her paws outstretched to the side, charging up reddish energy and began growing claws, an arrow-tipped tail and a big demonic pair of wings. She was shapeshifting into a demon, one which Hades found awfully familiar and feared.

"Oh no... Not Asmodia again," he muttered to himself, remembering her as the Queen of the Demons which took both he and the Empyreans to defeat, one of the tougher adversaries he had to face in the past. From the look of her eyes, she was seething with hatred and while her power was overwhelming her, corrupting her very being.

Once she was fully transformed into Asmodia, she resumed her wild rampage around the city, causing more considerable damage to everything around her. With a swipe of her claws, she tore down buildings into rubble in a matter of seconds, levelling the row of skyscrapers in her peripheral vision.

As things escalated to an uncontrolled level, he knew that something had to be done. He had to play his trump card, his ultimate plan to stop Iris. With no other way to match her power now, the only way he could do so was to transform into Empyrea. He outstretched his paws to the side as he shapeshifted, feeling the same overwhelming magnitude of power searing through his body like before, glimmering white with aura.

'This is it! I'm ready,' he thought to himself, preparing himself with a pep talk for the fight of his life, the obstacle unlike any he had faced before. 'Empyrea, grant me your powers.'

Chapter 7

(The Final Showdown)

Hades, as a shapeshifted form of Empyrea, flew up into the air to face Iris. In the air, both of them were ceaselessly staring at each other with an intense gaze and they were in a stance to begin an onslaught, observing each other's movement closely for an opportune strike.

"I didn't wanna have to do this, but you leave me no choice."

"There wasn't a choice to begin with!"

And without further delay, she began to claw at him, rapidly slashing his face. With Empyrea's power, it gave Hades the divine dexterity of movements, allowing him to dodge every deadly swing of the claws in a split second. While dodging, he could only hear the "whooshing" sounds of her razor-sharp claws slashing through the air.

However, while he was distracted in dodging her attacks, she swung her arrow-tipped tail and struck him in the gut, causing him to be vulnerable for a split second before a claw struck on the left side of his face with high impact. The force of her claws tossed him through several buildings before he eventually stopped in one of them.

Scrambling to his feet, he quickly shifted himself backwards, startled by the shadowy silhouette of Asmodia in the rays of light that shone in through the hole in the building while she was floating outside.

It was then he remembered how strong and fast she was when he and the Empyreans fought her. She was going to be a pain to deal with by himself without the help of his Empyreans counterparts. Even though she was only an imitative copy, she felt as though she had the powers of the original. Returning to the fray, he fought back physically, blocking all her claws and tails from making contact with his body. As she continued her unending fury, she added in her wings into her whirlwind of attacks, countering Hades attacks as he did with hers.

After a while fighting a comprehensive stalemate battle, he could see no way to change the odds of winning in a physical fight against Iris unless he sneaked in a magical spell. He blasted her out of the building with an immensely charged blast of energy unleashed from his paw. Astonished from the sudden cunning trick, she was breathing heavily from both the surprise of the attack and the torment that came after the fact, stopping herself midair to try to keep her body from flying backwards into buildings.

"Playing dirty, huh? It's just the way I like it! Let's take up a notch then!"

The demonic energy began to surge throughout her body and her eyes began to blaze like fire, red with fury. Her wings extended further and her tail remoulded itself, growing sharper with barbed edges. Hades, in Empyrea's image, followed suit and charged himself past the limit with tremendous amounts of Empyrean energy being unleashed, leaving his body to feel burning sensations from the scale of power he had in his grasps at that very moment.

They clashed once more, but this time, intense shockwaves of energy spewed out in every direction as the extreme ends of their power met. From below, it appeared as if they were fireworks as their magical energy spells exploded every time they collided.

Iris began to take their fight into a more exhilarating battle, teleporting everywhere to attempt to strike Hades' vital points with dark magical energy and her tail at every moment she could. He, too, teleported to dodge her blasts and attacks, but he held back his powers to give him time to strategize a way to defeat her.

With Empyrea's thinking and abilities in his grasp, he predicted the next location in which Iris would pop out at and shot an intense charge of Empyrean energy in the direction of her expected trajectory. As she reappeared, she was met with a blinding ball of energy, ramming her onto the asphalt roads below.

The impact shook the ground violently, creating a big crater in its wake and it could even be felt from the air above where Hades was. Following her fall was an Empyrean energy shockwave of intense proportions as her body reverted to her true form, levelling the surrounding buildings and remnants of them into dust in her proximity.

Hades flew down towards her, immediately running towards Iris' side and holding her in his arms.

"H-Hades?"

"Iris…" He began to tear as he lifted her body in his paws, knowing what was going to unfold before him.

"IR-15, obey my command, you defiant fool!" Maverick demanded, shooting cascading beams of energy and causing her to suffer under the torturous surge of Empyrean energy directed into her body. Resisting the intense hypnotic beam from above, she wiped the tears from her cheeks and climbed off Hades' arms, standing up and tramping her way towards Maverick's ship with tempestuous feelings of anger and revenge.

"No… Not this time!" She shouted in resistance. She mustered all of the remaining energy she had left in her body and summoned a huge mass of energy, hurling it towards his ship, causing it to explode midair on contact and its debris raining down around them. Afterwards, she collapsed back into Hades' arms, unable to move anymore. Her body was burnt-out of Empyrean energies, some parts of her body scorched by the very energies that once ran in her veins.

"Well, that settles it," she said with a wistful smile, touching his cheek lovingly. "Hades, it was fun while it lasted. Until next time…"

Her paw dropped from his face after a moment of silence. Hades leaned his forehead against hers as she turned cold and motionless. Gradually, her body began to fade away from existence, dissipating into the air like the glowing embers of fire as she turned back into the Empyrean energies used to create her. As her body disappeared from her physical state, only the hypnosis collar remained in his paws.

He began sobbing as he stared at the collar and sank deep into his thoughts. Losing a friend who was close to him was heart-rending and he wished he could have done anything else to stop it. While he sat on the ground in grief, he could see something shining in the smouldering debris of the destroyed ship. It was the Empyrean Shard, still attached to the wrecked remote control.

He wiped off his tears and began to shift away all the debris covering the remote. He lifted it from the ground, detaching the Shard from the remote. Inspecting it in his paws and glancing at the wreck around him, he knew what he needed to do next.

He had unlimited Empyrean power in his paws with the aid of the Shard. Immediately, he slowed time down to a halt, providing all the time he needed to undo all the damage and destruction left on the city.

Bit by bit, he fixed up everything from the damaged buildings to the holes in the streets, make sure that the damage incurred by their clash was all gone. Next, he cleared out all the wreckage he considered extraterrestrial to the humans or items which seemed to stick out of the ordinary, trawling around the city for any more remnants or debris of SAIRO so that it could appear as if nothing unusual had happened.

While scanning the city for debris, he could see SAIRO agents in the midst of leaving their cars with various weapons but they were still in the time-pause. This was a worrying sign for both he and Casey. Since time had stopped for him, he had the opportunity to teleport the SAIRO agents and their cars together at another corner of the city to delay their progress to move towards him and to wipe their memories out later in one fell swoop.

After clearing up all of the extraneous remains, he searched for Casey, eventually finding her standing along a crosswalk. As he unpaused time, he informed her of the situation about the SAIRO agents being in the city and they might be in danger.

Unfortunately, where they were was close to where the agents were teleported to. They could see the agents running towards them with pistols and various weapons, preparing to arrest them if they did not do anything.

"Casey, I'll need to erase everything that anyone saw here before we go, including the SAIRO's memory of me and Iris, which means, you might not remember me at all. This is necessary for the timeline on Earth to resume normally."

"But-"

"There's no time to lose. Trust me," he assured, putting a paw on her shoulder. "It's for the better."

Hades closed his eyes as he held up the Shard, which emitted a blinding explosion of light, wiping the memories of everyone present during the clash to prevent any further panic in the city. Once it was finished, he opened his eyes and saw Casey staring blankly at him. At the sight of Hades, she smiled and walked slowly towards him.

Without hesitation, she lifted him from the ground and hugged him, nuzzling him for a bit. He knew from her actions that her memory remained throughout the process of the memory wipe. With their friendship so strong, even their memories could withstand the effects of the spell, as if being connected by an intangible tether.

When everything returned to normal, Hades quickly teleported both he and Casey back to her home to prevent the SAIRO agents from spotting them again. However, once they returned home, she questioned where Iris was, seeing that they were the only ones who made it out of the city safely.

Hades' ears drooped and his head fell low, explaining that she was manipulated to the point that her physical being could not handle it, disappearing forever without a trace left to find. Casey, too, was saddened.

Together, they built a grave at the base of the tree in her garden as a commemoration of the memories that they spent while she was around, leaving flowers and pictures of the three of them beside the grave.

As soon as it was built, they went to the swings and swung mournfully with their heads pointed downwards. Hades gazed intently at the Shard now in the grasps of his paw, realising that he was returning to Xenia soon, which was something he longed for what seemed to be an eternity. But it was a matter of fact that he had to part ways with Casey and their time together was going to end eventually.

He kept it to himself until the appropriate time to break the news to her and held it back as a secret for several weeks on end.

Chapter 8

(Returning Home)

As the final days were spent with each other, Hades would shapeshift into a human to do activities he would never get to do once he left the world. Using an old, tattered photo of Casey's father, he transformed to change his appearance to copy the looks he had when he was a child. Surprised but entertained by his shapeshifting abilities, Casey's father allowed him to take his childhood looks as a disguise anywhere they wanted to go.

They spent their remaining time in theme parks, movies and all sorts of shopping areas, having fun as they teased and played around with each other. Memories were created and their bonds strengthened as they adventures around the town area.

Casey, in her mind, saw Hades as a close friend, wanting him to stay with her forever to make her life more interesting and happier. But, little did she know that during those experiences, he kept dropping subtle hints on his eventual departure, but she did not seem to catch on to any of his clues.

Two nights before the supposed return, he had visions of the locations and exact time he was to be present for him to travel home, seeing himself in a clearing beside Empyrea, holding the Shard in his paw. Although he did not understand what he was supposed to do, he knew that he was going home soon.

As he awoke the next morning, he sighed with both with ears directed downwards, knowing that he would have to disclose the secret sooner or later. Upon revealing this fact truthfully to Casey, she was filled with mixed emotions - happy because he was returning to his friends; saddened by the fact that they were parting ways and she might never see him again. Staying calm and composed about leaving his side, she requested one more thing - to tag along and see him off.

On the day itself, Hades had the location in mind, bringing her through the forest past the big lake of the park onto a gravel-littered hill path. The path took them up into a forest clearing, where some of the stones and flora was positioned in a bizarre way. There were stone obelisks with runic hieroglyphs, six of them to be exact, forming a hexagon at the boundaries of the clearing around a ring of vibrantly coloured flowers.

In the middle of the ring sat a white, glowing spirit with a long tail and several distinctive purple markings. It was Empyrea, who was awaiting his arrival as shown in the vision he saw in the series of dreams from the nights before.

She turned to Hades, nodding in a silent tacit acknowledge of what was to come next.

"Hades, your companionship with Leo is not only connected through the heart but also through your souls, stronger than even the boundless distances between the Multiverse are unable to sever, just as you bonded with your friend, Casey. Come forth and reconnect physically with him, one paw to where your heart is and the other, to the heavens with the Shard," she instructed, moving to his side to watch the procedures to ensure that it went smoothly.

As he positioned his left paw at his heart and held up the Empyrean Shard with his right, he could see Casey observing from the side, clasping her hands in hope that she could see him again. The Shard began to glow progressively, turning into a radiant blue flare of light which strangely felt warm and comforting, an enjoyable feeling for those around him.

When the light of the Shard stopped emanating the blinding lights, he could see a dimensional rift open in front of him and blustery winds blew around him. Through the pulsating portal, he saw a familiar silhouette emerging slowly from the rift, someone he had known for a very long time. He smiled and knew immediately who it was when he exited the rift.

"Foxy?" Leo called out, his eyes gaping at Hades in disbelief.

"Leo!" Without hesitation, he leapt up onto his body and hugged him. Behind him came the rest of the Empyreans, who came around to join the hug, feeling the familiar warmth of his friends he yearned for after so long. As he was released from the hug, they did some catching up on some of the things they did. But Hades still had one more thing to finish before they returned.

His head fell low and his ears drooped behind him as he shuffled slowly towards Casey.

"I guess this is it for now. I promise never to forget you. Goodbye Casey."

Casey brought him in for yet another hug, tears streaming down her face. "I'm going to miss you too, Hades. I gotta admit, you've been one of the most interesting foxes I met in my entire life."

Once she let go, Hades beckoned her to bend down before cupping his paws around her ear, "it's alright, I might find another way here to visit you again."

Before he left, she wrapped the red bandana he used to wear around his neck, telling him that it was something for him to remember her by. She wiped her tears off to try to wear her best smile for his departure. Despite being contented yet saddened, she waved goodbye with a beaming smile as he and the rest of the Empyreans entered the rift, sealing up after they passed through.

Part 2 Short Story

Saving Iris

Each story has its ending, be it a happy or sad one or maybe a mixture of feelings. For Hades, he felt that it could not be the end of his story because he could not accept how it came to be. With his ingenuity and his new dimension travelling ability learned through accessing Leo's most recent memories, he was about to make a difference, another chance for the better.

While Leo was sleeping soundly, Hades sneaked into his room and took the Shard. 'Ah, it's great to feel the warmth of the Shard again,' he thought he held it in his paws. Stepping out of his room to the balcony, he waved it in a circle to open up a rift back to Casey's room on Earth. As he passed through the rift, he fell onto Casey who was reading a book on her bed, landing directly onto her lap. His sudden appearance startled her as it was a literal drop-in on her.

"Hades? What a surprise!" Her eyes widened in surprise as her hopes of seeing meeting him again became true, instinctively bringing him into her embrace. "Why are you here at this moment?"

"Well... do you remember... Iris?" He hesitated for a moment, pausing in between his words, hoping to not bring her mood down by the recollection of the past.

Nevertheless, her smile gradually turned into a frown as she nodded.

"Don't be sad, Casey. I'm here to change the past to save Iris before anything happened to her. You know, some stories like this one can't have sad endings so-"

"You're time travelling?"

"Yep! That's what I intend to do here!"

"Cool!" Her face lit up as a sense of optimism returned to her. "Good luck and bring her back!"

Utilizing the Shard's power once more, in addition to Leo's power in which he 'borrowed', he travelled back to the time when Iris turned ill, transporting himself into the kitchen right beside the living room where she was.

Peeking from behind the walls that divided both rooms, he saw his past-self holding Iris in his paws with a look of distress slapped onto his face. But, to save Iris, he would have to break the rules of spacetime to appear in front of his past-self. However, despite his eventual and inevitable decision to break it, Empyrea allowed it, watching in silence from the sidelines, veiled in her invisible state.

As he revealed himself to them from behind the wall, both Hades, past and present, gazed at each other vacantly. His past-self was confused at what was presented in front of him. Casey, who had just rushed into the living room to Iris' aid, had a similar reaction and just froze with her mouth opened agape. Hades was momentarily stunned, hesitating to introduce himself to them.

"Hello Hades, I'm you from the future, here to prevent you from losing Iris."

"You can't be me. How can I even trust you?" He doubted, thinking that his future self might be one of his enemies.

Instinctively, his past-self pounced on him, pinning him to the ground just in case.

"Ah!" Hades exclaimed as he fell backwards. "W-Wait a second! I am you and you are me, so we share the same memories and abilities too. Have a look!" He promptly placed a paw on his equal's forehead, allowing him to 'view' his memories and be informed of what was to come before it happened. As the realisation hit him, he decided that he would chip in to help in any way.

With a plan in mind, he told his past-self, first of all, not to reveal that he even existed to anyone other than their small group. Next, he informed Casey that he would just hide in her backpack and execute his plan stealthily, even without her detection, leaving the rest of the variables remaining similar. He requested that she kept her bag slightly unzipped for him to peep through and so that he could slip out easily later when the moment was right.

And as time went on, they were eventually escorted into Maverick's laboratory. Every step made by Casey was like an earthquake to Hades as it shook him up and down and side to side inside the bag, but it was endurable for him in comparison to other similar situations. He peeked out from the unzipped portion of the bag intermittently to check on their location every few seconds, waiting for them to reach the internal section of the laboratory.

When they reached the main laboratory, he sneaked out of Casey's backpack to bide his time for the appropriate moment to get into gear and stop Maverick. He skulked around the laboratory, hidden in the shadows while he clambered up the pipelines above to spy on them, giving him the viewpoint of a wider area for observation.

As Maverick began to charge the chamber up with Empyrean energy, both Casey and past Hades were trapped in the same glass dome, just like before. Once Iris' chamber was fully charged, Maverick removed the Shard which was connected to the energy canister of his re-energization chamber, already preparing to grab his remote control in his reach.

Right at the moment he inserted the Shard into his remote control, Hades leapt through the air and snatched the Shard out of his hand, somersaulting before landing right in front of him.

"Why you little rat-" he yelled furiously as he whipped out an energy pistol, shooting plasma beams as they ran around the laboratory. Each beam was so lethally intense that it could perforate solid metal with each hit, leaving the walls full of holes appearing like cheese. "Come back with my power source!"

The chase continued for minutes, eventually leading to Hades positioning himself in front of the glass dome, taunting Maverick by shaking his hind and tail about mischievously. And with a shot of plasma, he dodged the deadly beam and both Casey and his past-self were freed as it hit the surface of the glass, turning the glass into bits of sand.

With two Shards in his possession, he pointed both of them in front of him. Using both as though they were chalk, he drew an illuminated circle of Empyrean magic in the air. As he approached, he turned the circle into a rift and sent the circular rift whirling towards Maverick, whisking him into a random dimension. Hades then trapped him inside permanently as the rift was sealed with the aid of the two Shards, leaving him with no escape routes from the other side of the Multiverse.

The next thing he needed to do was to calibrate the "re-energization" chamber into an energy-stabilization chamber so that Iris would not dissipate into energy like before. He told both Casey and his past-self not to fret as he was going to transform into Maverick momentarily to access his mind.

As he transformed, he shared thoughts with Maverick and slowly but surely, he rewired the whole system. "Put these here, and these there..." He said while inserting the Shard into the energy canister, unplugging valves and replugging them, lastly changing the settings of the machine. "And... Voila, one Empyrean Energy Quantum stabilizer ready to go." Once the customisations were completed, he reverted to his true form and initialised the contraption's process.

"Ding!" The chamber sounded as it fulfilled its purpose.

"Iris is ready for serving!" Hades giggled cheekily from the side, adding this last bit of customisations to the contraption, making it seem as though Iris just came fresh from the oven. The next step was to open the chamber to get her out.

After a bit of poking around the buttons of the chamber, Hades unlocked it and lifted the chamber glass to give Iris some fresh air. She opened her eyes and blinked, rubbing her eyes along with a high-pitched yawn and stretched as she sat up in the chamber. As she turned towards them, she was bewildered by the fact that there were two Hades and her eyes immediately widened.

"What the-? Am I seeing double?"

Hades explained that she was indeed seeing double, just that one of them came from the future to save her from disappearing. And with a double explanation in unison from both Hades and his double, she quickly understood everything and thank Hades for saving her. Once her hypnosis collar was removed, she was finally safe from all harm.

"Oh, before I go, Hades, take the Shard and wait out a couple of months. When the time is right, you'll of where and when to be present for your return." Once Hades passed the Shard to his past-self, his mission was complete.

While travelling back into the future in the timeline, he decided to drop by to check on both Iris and his past-self before returning to his own time. Observing both Iris and his past-self from the roof, he began to eavesdrop on several conversations as time went by. However, there was one of them in particular which caused him to be downcast.

His past-self held Iris' paw, sitting and watching the sunset from the branches of the tree in Casey's backyard. They were discussing about the return trip back to Xenia.

"Y-you really wanna stay on Earth?" Hades' past-self questioned. She nodded in response.

"Since I was created here, I feel that something is compelling me to stay. It's like my roots have already been implanted into this world. And if I were to leave, I'd feel disconnected. And, I wanna remain here with Casey to make her happy, like what I wished for that night when I first came here. It makes me feel complete. I guess it's kind of a spiritual thing..."

Hades continued to watch them chat until they fell asleep, lying down paw in paw. At this point, he knew that Iris would be separated from him forever. He was crushed on the fact that after all the effort he had put in, she would still prefer to be apart from him. Empyrea, who had trailed him from the start and sat quietly in the dark, appeared from her invisible veil beside him. She wrapped a paw around his shoulder and he leaned his head against her shoulder.

"Let her go, Hades. This is destiny, and destiny doesn't change. If you love her, you should set her free."

With a stream of tears rolling down his cheeks, he turned back to have a final look at them, seeing them sleeping peacefully together.

"Destiny has other plans for you, Hades. And don't worry, love would always find its way around. I have a plan for you too, but let's return to Xenia for now."

She opened a rift directly back to Xenia and both returned. As Hades travelled back to Xenia, he knew he was returning empty-pawed, but additionally feeling content that things have indeed worked out for the better, ending the way he wanted it, the more favourable ending.

The End

Character Biographies

Name: Leo Stargazer

Description: He is a Leopard Felinean of Felineatius, the planet of cats. As the leader of the Empyreans, he was mostly serious and will try his best to achieve what is set out for him, even if it means he has to go through hardships. He is loyal and selfless, well-organised and a great leader of the Empyreans.

Background origins: He was given powers by Empyrea and a task to find the others like him. The Empyrean Shard, a fragment of the Empyrean Comet that once flew through the void of space, gave him the powers of magic as the first chosen Empyrean. Over time, his powers grew stronger, and eventually, he survived the destruction of Felineatius by a miracle of magic. He was later rescued and taken into care by the former leader of the Intergalactic Federation of Xenia, Basileus, as he was supposedly the last of his kind and needed all the protection he could ever have. With guidance from the Xenian mages, his power was fully developed much so that he was able to defend himself. When he grew up, he became one of the most knowledgeable and well-renowned astronomers in the Intergalactic Federation.

Empyrean Abilities: Energy spells, flight, teleportation, Empyrean magic capable of both space and time travel, temporal-based abilities, interdimensional rifting

Name: Hades (Part 2)

Description: He is a purple fox of Frisktonia, the planet of small critters. He is always cheerful and energetic, and most importantly, a close and intimate companion of Leo. He is also nicknamed "Foxy" by Leo as a joke because he was treated like a pet before it was caught on and was used by Leo to address him ever since. He is a sweet tooth and is often coax with cookies, namely vanilla or strawberry flavoured ones. However, he does not like to be regarded as a pet, being very sensitive and particular about the term.

Background origins: As a Frisktonian, he was frequently encountered with problems of Xenian hunters who wanted to capture him and sell him as a pet illegally. Being one of the hardest to catch critters who was an expert at hiding from them, they named him Hades, the unseen Frisktonian fox. However, he was successfully smuggled to Xenia by hunters but he managed to escape their grasp at the very last minute, eventually finding his way into Leo's life.

Empyrean Abilities: Shapeshifting and ability to learn by accessing the memories of whatever he transforms into and thinking like them, even the language they speak. Through his shapeshifting, he is to use their powers, if any is present, and manipulate as and when he needs certain types of abilities. He is also able to allow others to view his visions or memories through the touch of the mind.

Name: Ignis Verglas

Description: She is a Sylvian Hare orphan with Ecru(light brown)-coloured fur of the Sylvian Kingdom. Being highly imaginative and energetic, she is sometimes shy and emotional. Being a Sylvian, her ears are sensitive enough to eavesdrop on a whisper from far away. Her voice has an European accent to it.

Background origins: She was taken into care by elementals on Elementus, her name was derived from her proficiency in fire and ice elemental magic - known as the "Frosted Fire" of Elementus.

Empyrean Abilities: Elemental manipulation (primarily fire and ice) and flight

Name: Kadyn Flynx

Description: She is a Felinean Lynx from Felineatius. She is stubborn, adaptable, a risk-taker and she is Leo's life partner. Her voice has an Arabian accent to it.

Background origins: She was an orphan captured from her home by Asmodia and the demons for experimentations. After a few days of being captured, she attempted to escape and eventually got herself stranded in a desert planet, Siliconia. Growing up under the care of its inhabitants, she was trained in their ways as bandits of the dunes and was given special lightweight scimitars passed down through the generations.

Empyrean Abilities: Superspeed in movement and attacks, ability to withstand extreme climates and adverse conditions, rapid regeneration

Name: Kyudo

Description: He is a grey wolf of Pinophyto, the Planet of the Pines. He is calm and collected, resourceful, intelligent and most of all, nature-loving. His voice has a Japanese accent to it.

Background origins: He was the former leader of the Wind Strider until he passed his leadership to his son. Born in a village of archery, he was named after the martial arts of the bow. He is an archer of great skill and wields an Ornate bow bequeathed by his elder. Being close to nature, he loves to spend time in the woods, peacefully by himself, sipping tea while sitting on a nearby stump.

Empyrean Abilities: Deadshot aim, capable of materialising any kind of arrows at his will with Empyrean magic, even arrows created from pure Empyrean energy for stronger adversaries.

Name: Seiche

Description: He is a Salamandarian inhabitant of Thropicthyde, the planet which is a paradise for surfers. He is frivolous and likes to have fun, but sometimes arrogant with his surfing skills as he has done death-defying feats in his youth on his home planet, conquering the roughest waves in the galaxies. His voice has a Hawaiian accent to it, with several accents and jargons in his speeches.

Background origins: Seiche was named after the constantly undulating waves along the seaside. He was, and still is, one of the best surfers around, taking on one of the hardest areas to surf and successfully completing it while developing his new powers, the scales on his body. His scales, infused with Empyrean energy and gifted by Empyrea, helps him to surf, in combat and other activities of all sorts.

Empyrean Abilities: He is able to use his scales to construct weapons, shields or other items via the use of Empyrean magic; His scales are also used as explosive projectiles and a rapid scale regeneration to prevent the loss of his scale "ammunition" or "armour".

Name: Empyrea

Description: She is spirit from Spiritus, wise and solemn, she only speaks for however much that she needed to be revealed, keeping her secrets of the events in the spacetime continuum concealed in her mind.

Background origins: She is origin of Empyrean magic and the one to choose the Empyreans to fulfil the Prophecy, "with the heavenly powers, the six Empyreans shall unite, lighting the darkness with unparalleled might". Before transmuting her intangible soul into a spirit of Spiritus, she was a spectral being after the Empyrean Comet exploded. To make sure that the path of destiny does not move astray, she observes from all corners of the Universe with her powers and shares her words of wisdom to the Empyreans in time of need.

Empyrean Abilities: She is able to use her magic in any way, shape or form, depending on the situation; her Empyrean magic is limitless and unparalleled compared to most of the Empyreans.

Other Characters
Name: "Paws" Paulson

Description: He is brown bear scientist of the Intergalactic Federation of Xenia, he is smart and innovative, resourceful but he does not like to leave the laboratories. Although a side character, he contributes a lot to help the Empyreans accomplish their goals smoothly and efficiently.

Background origins: He nicknamed "Paws" because of the first half of his name and the fact that he was able to invent gadgets and technological upgrades dexterously with his paws.

Name: Wensleydale 'Mousse' Hamilton

Description: He is a Xenian bespectacled mouse in a lab coat, arrogant (at times) about his achievements and his bloodline. He is often called by the name Wendale or Dale in short. He is much smaller and shorter compared to the rest of the characters, being around the waist height of Leo if compared to him. Typically, he likes to speak in lengthy, scientific jargon. His voice is high pitched and has European accents.

Background origins: He is a scientist who researches the properties of different dimensions, a Dimensional Delver of the Federation.

Name: Brander, the Bovinean

Description: He is a heavily-built Bovinean inhabitant of the destroyed Horizon, a blacksmith and a good friend of Wendale.

However, he can be too friendly and might hurt others without knowing. His speaks with Irish-like accents.

Name: Faye, the Vulpine

Description: A white, vulpine orphan who came under the care of Brander, seeking safeguard while she grew. She has psychic abilities that developed during the destruction of Horizon. Her powers include telepathy, psychokinetic manipulation, mind and memory reading. She is somewhat mischievous and likes to use her powers on others. Her story will continue...

Abilities: Psychic power manipulation which includes, levitation and flight, hypnosis, telekinesis and telepathy

Name: The Great Lezaros

Description: Draped in a dark purple cloak, he travels through dimensions to rule over the beings. His motives are a mystery, but he has grown a certain sort of hatred against the Empyreans. *Read the story (Part 1) for more information.*

Abilities: Dark magic manipulation, teleportation, flight, interdimensional travel, elemental manipulation

*Most of the context of biographies in <u>Part 1</u> is with reference to the previous book and its short stories.

<u>Part 2</u>
Name: Casey, the Human

Background: She is 12 and she often likes to "assist" her father in the Wildlife Sanctuary to see all the different animals. Being playful and mischievous, she would sometimes prod the animals in her father's wildlife sanctuary. As childish as she might seem, she is also vigilant and watchful of any injured animals there would be on the road as her father drives her around, caring for any of them when needed like a mother.

Name: Iris "IR-15", the Clone

Description: Mauve-coloured clone of Hades, created by the scientists of SAIRO. She shares similar traits to him, along with similar Empyrean abilities, memories and behaviours

Background: Hades was cloned to create Iris as an experimental subject. *Read the story (Part 2) for more information...*

Name: Asmodia, the Demon (From the previous book)

Description: She is a red-skinned demon with glowing yellow eyes, wearing a black suit of armour. She has wings and an arrowhead tipped tail, both in which she uses in complement with her clawed hands during combat. She is especially skilled in both physical and mystical combat, being one of the strongest adversaries that the Empyreans had to deal with in the past (the previous story).

Background: She is the Queen of the demons, also known as Asmodians, on her home planet.

*Some of the characters have paws instead of hands, in representation of their childish characteristic traits or just their particular species. These characters include: "Paws" Paulson, Wendale, Hades, Ignis (and the Sylvians), Faye and Iris.

*Most characters mentioned in this section are anthropomorphic.

Certain information here is with reference to the previous book and/or additional stories along with which can be found here: https://bit.ly/2qCnAX3

Lightning Source UK Ltd.
Milton Keynes UK
UKHW012310270120
357710UK00003B/149